Brandon's Posse

Brandon's Posse

RAY HOGAN

Sagebrush
Large Print Westerns

Library of Congress Cataloging in Publication Data

Hogan, Ray, 1908-1998.
    Brandon's posse / Ray Hogan.
        p.   cm.
    ISBN 1-57490-172-9 (alk. paper)
    1. Large type books.   I. Title.
[PS3558.O3473B72   1999]
813'.54—dc21   98-48132
                                                                        CIP

Cataloguing in Publication Data is available from
the British Library and the National Library of Australia.

Sagebrush Large Print Westerns are published in the United
States and Canada by Thomas T. Beeler, Publisher, Box 659,
Hampton Falls, New Hampshire 03844-0659. ISBN 1-57490-172-9

Published in the United Kingdom, Eire, and the Republic of South
Africa by Isis Publishing Ltd, 7 Centremead, Osney Mead, Oxford
OX2 0ES England. ISBN 0-7531-6002-1

Published in Australia and New Zealand by Australian Large Print
Audio & Video Pty Ltd, 17 Mohr Street, Tullamarine, Victoria, 3043,
Australia. ISBN 1-86442-266-1

Manufactured in the United States of America by BookCrafters, Inc.

Brandon's Posse

CHAPTER 1

IT HAD BEEN ONE HELL OF A DAY SO FAR. STARBUCK had risen early after an uncomfortable night in a dry camp, scraped together a breakfast of coffee, fried meat and grease-soaked bread that was as hard as a stonemason's chisel. Then, just as he was about to down the mess, an erratic gust of the persistent wind that had plagued him for three days garnished it all with a generous topping of sand. Disgusted, he had dumped the spider's contents, gulped the coffee and ridden on.

Right in keeping with that inauspicious beginning, the sorrel had been contrary and hard-mouthed and was earning the spurs and the harsh hand on the leathers he was getting as they moved, teeth to the wind, steadily southwest across a vast, rolling mesa.

It was no consoling thought that Santa Fe, his planned destination where he hoped to find or else learn something of value concerning his brother Ben, for whom he'd searched so long, was still many days away—on the yonder side and opposite end of the dark, towering mountains he could see dimly in the dust-hazed distance.

The ashes and charred remnants of Babylon where he had served briefly as marshal of that riotous colony of gambling and women were behind him, as were Dodge City, Cheyenne, Las Cruces, El Paso, Tucson—all the other places he'd visited in his ceaseless quest for the brother, who in anger had fled the family home in Ohio a decade ago.

He had found only cold trails wherever he went and very possibly he would fare no better in the ancient

1

capital of the *Conquistadores*, but as always he must try, must know. Ben was somewhere, and someday he would find him—and then the search would end. Until that moment, however, he led the life of a wanderer, a drifter, one dedicated to hunting for a man he hadn't seen since boyhood and likely would not recognize should they come face to face.

A blast of fine sand whipped at him. Shawn swore irritably, brushed at his eyes and lips, spat. The gelding, stung also by the dry particles, jerked his head nervously, shied off the faint trail they were following.

Starbuck brought the sorrel back into line, glanced ahead. They were breaking off the mesa and dropping into a wide area of buttes and arroyos littered with rabbitbrush, cactus and other rank growth. Dust devils stirred into frantic motion by the capricious wind: spun across the more open flats, leaped intervening obstacles and spiraled on toward the limitless prairie. He sighed. Matters were not going to get any better.

Guiding the sorrel to a break in the low wall of the arroyo, he swung the big red horse into it. The gelding started down, felt the soil give way under his front hooves. He tried to pull back. Instantly a ten-foot-long section of the bank broke off. The sorrel bunched, sprang, eyes rolling wildly, ears laid flat. He struck on bent knees, went down on his left side. Starbuck, barely able to throw himself clear of the thrashing horse, went fall length into a mass of brittle-stalked snakeweed.

Cursing, wrists and face smarting from the scratches he'd received, Starbuck scrambled to his feet and whirled to the sorrel. Relief moved through him. The horse was up, appeared to be unhurt by the fall. Dusting himself with his hat, he crossed to where the gelding waited.

Shawn swore again. A steady dripping sound told him that his canteen had been caught under the sorrel and crushed by his weight. It had emptied itself quickly through a burst seam and now contained only a few drops.

Unhooking the container from the saddle, he held it overhead to catch the small amount yet remaining, and then tossing it aside, took up the sorrel's reins. He moved forward leading the gelding, eyes watching closely for any indication of a limp. The horse showed no signs of having lamed himself. Grunting in satisfaction, Shawn stepped back into the saddle.

He remained motionless, staring out across the windy landscape. There should be a stream, or at least a spring, somewhere along the hills that he could see in the distance—but it would take the remainder of the day to reach that point and by then he would be plenty thirsty. He shrugged, a tall, gray-eyed man not long out of boyhood in years but well into that phase by the reckoning of trouble and experience, and lifted the reins. He'd live through it, he'd make it. Hell, he had to. There was no other choice.

Roweling the sorrel lightly, he moved on into the arroyo, his mood blacker now from one more irritating incident, his impatience heightened by another of the needless, uncalled-for tribulations that were riding him. . . . There were days when a man should just stay in his blankets.

Near noon the wind finally died, and with a show of dark clouds gathering in the west, he halted to rest the sorrel. He decided against eating; with no water it would only increase the thirst that was making itself felt. Restless, he stalled out a full hour for the sake of the gelding, and then climbing back onto his hull, pressed

3

on.

Shortly he was out of the arroyo and again on a broad, rolling mesa sparsely covered with a thin grass that showed gray in its need for rain. But that was due to end, he guessed, once more eyeing the thickening clouds; a storm was in the offing, and with good luck, should strike sometime during the night.

He hoped the hell he'd have reached a town or a ranch by then; he was in no mood to get soaking wet and besides, the way things were going, he'd like as not get struck by lightning or come a-cropper from some other bit of misfortune.

A time later he pulled in the sorrel. A quarter-mile on, squatted along the first hint of rising land that lifted gracefully to the mountains beyond, was a homesteader's holdings—a sagging, slanted roof shack, two or three dilapidated sheds, a corral, a small stretch of cultivated ground and a water well.

Brushing at his cracked lips, Starbuck urged the gelding on, pointing for the circle of stones and water bucket at the side of the bleak little structures. A door banged in the warm hush. A figure appeared and the afternoon's quiet was further shattered by the deafening blast of a shotgun.

Starbuck hauled up short as pellets spurted dust only a stride in front of the sorrel. Anger rocking through him, he raised both hands, palms forward and stared. It was a woman. She was wearing a ragged and soiled housedress of sleazy gray, and her hair, unkempt and tangled, straggled down over her leathery face and neck, but it did not conceal the fierceness and the fright that filled her eyes.

"Hold on! Just looking for a drink of water," he called.

"You ain't getting it here—'cause you ain't stopping!" the woman yelled, waving the shotgun menacingly.

The cocked hammer of the as yet unfired barrel of the old ten-gauge looked as big as a man's thumb. Starbuck forced a thin smile.

"Mean you no harm, ma'am," he said, trying to keep the edge from his tone. "Horse of mine fell, busted my canteen. Been most of the day without water."

"Ain't a damn whit to me—keep moving!"

Starbuck shrugged. No one in his right mind would argue with a frightened woman holding a cocked scattergun in her hands—thirsty or not.

"Yes, ma'am," he said, lowering his arms. "I'm going. Sure would appreciate a little of that water, however."

"You'll find some—about an hour down the way. . . Wolf Crossing."

Shawn paused. "That a town?"

"Now, what do you think it is—a Sunday sociable?"

"No, ma'am," Starbuck muttered, and simmering under his hat, doubled back to the trail.

Once out of the shotgun's range, he relaxed, took a deep breath. Anger still plucked at him, but the moments were tempered now by the thought that he was coming into a settlement where he could satisfy his needs and find comfort for the night.

It was a fair-sized town he noted with further pleasure as he rounded a shoulder of rock and caught sight of the structures nestled in the cove of a steeply rising mountain. He could see three or four two-storied buildings, the steeple of a church, as well as a short main street along which business houses stood shoulder to shoulder on either side. Residences were scattered

5

about it all in a loose circle.

A splash of silver behind the structures marked a stream and for a time he was tempted to cut off from the road be was following and go first to the creek and satisfy his thirst, but he decided against it. Better to pull up to the first saloon he came to, get his fill of water and then treat himself to a drink of rye whiskey. Afterwards he'd see to the sorrel, get a room at the hotel and think about a good meal.

Shortly he turned into the end of the street, noted curiously the number of persons gathered in front of a low-roofed, sprawling, building that bore the sign SQUARE DOLLAR SALOON, and slanted toward its hitchrack.

Several men, listening to a dark, thickset individual wearing the town marshal's star, turned to glance at him as he rode the gelding up to the rack and then returned their attention to the lawman. Some sort of trouble in Wolf Crossing, Shawn concluded as he swung from the saddle—trouble he aimed to stay clear of. Brushing at the dust stiffening his face, he glanced idly along the street . . . GRAND CENTRAL HOTEL Wm. Gooch, Prop . . . ORY JONES GENERAL MERCHANDISE . . . STRATTON DRY GOODS & SUPPLIES . . . L. A. MARBERRY, M.D. . . JOSHUA WILLIS LAWYER . . . THE ANTELOPE CAFE. . . .

"Be a cold day in hell when them Paradise jaspers gets any help from this town!"

At the sound of the words coming from a man close by, Starbuck turned. They had been directed to the lawman, who wagged his head slowly while he stroked the thick mustache that covered his lip.

"I'm the law around here. I'm obliged to do my duty."

6

"You ain't always felt that way about this here duty of yours, Brandon," another voice in the crowd said. "How's it come you're thinking so strong about it now? Been a few times when folks needed—"

"Always done what I figured was right—"

"Sure—right for you!"

"Makes no difference now. I'm asking for a posse—for volunteers."

"You got yourself three," the speaker said, and laughed.

Brandon half turned, cast an indifferent look at the men standing behind him—a Negro clad in ordinary cowhand garb, a slumped puncher with the drawn, haggard features of a sobering alcoholic, and a slightly built, pale individual whose checked suit and small hat marked him as a newcomer from somewhere east of the Mississippi.

"Need more'n them."

Shawn wrapped the sorrel's reins around the crossbar of the rack and turned to make his way to the saloon's porch. The gelding shied to one side. Instantly a man cursed.

"What the hell you doing? Goddam jughead of yours stepped on my foot!"

Shawn rounded the hindquarters of the gelding, faced the two punchers standing there. His mood had improved little since early morning and the edge of his temper was sharp.

"Reckon my horse is begging your pardon," he said drily.

"The hell you say!" the taller of the pair snapped. "How about the jackass that's riding him?"

It was the ultimate, crowning episode of an arduous day. The balled fist of Starbuck's left arm lashed out,

7

caught the puncher flush on the nose. A fraction of a second later his right scored with deadly precision on the jaw. The man staggered, began to sink as his knees buckled. His partner yelled, reached for the pistol on his hip. Starbuck's left hand swept down, came up smoothly. Sunlight glinted off the barrel of his leveled forty-five.

"My advice—forget it," he said quietly.

The rider, half bent, palm wrapped around the weapon still in its holster, glanced about at the hushed crowd and then straightened slowly. His fingers relaxed their grip, slid away.

"Sure," he murmured almost inaudibly "sure" and shifted his eyes to his partner. "Whatever you say."

Shawn jammed his pistol back into its leather, shrugged and, ignoring the man, moved on toward the porch of the Square Dollar. Wolf Crossing was about as unfriendly a town as he'd ever ridden into—but he guessed maybe it was him; he wasn't feeling particularly neighborly himself.

CHAPTER 2

THE BARTENDER, A PAUNCHY, BALDING MAN WITH round eyes and a trailing mustache, was standing inside the doorway. He turned as Shawn entered, hurried to get in behind the counter which was immediately adjacent to the batwings.

"What'll it be?"

From habit, Starbuck glanced around the semidark room. It was deserted. Leaning against the bar, he nodded, pushed his hat to the back of his head. The edge had not faded entirely from his voice.

"Rye . . . some water first."

The balding man set a stone pitcher and a tumbler on the counter before Shawn, reached for a shot glass and a bottle, covertly studying him all the while. It was as if he were calculating the wisdom of launching into his usual companionable conversation with strangers.

Starbuck solved the problem for him. Downing a second glass of water, he jerked his thumb in the direction of the street.

"What's going on out there?"

The bartender's brow pulled into a frown. "Been a killing," he said, filling the shot glass with liquor and placing it in front of Shawn. "Four men. The marshal's trying to make up a posse and go after the outlaws that done it."

"Not having much luck, seems."

"He won't around here."

Starbuck's brows lifted. "I figured he was the local lawman."

"He is—but he won't be after next month. Folks just plain ain't got no use for Harry Brandon. Election's coming up and he won't get another term."

Shawn stirred. "It's still the law. If he needs help people ought to give it to him."

The bartender's shoulders twitched. "Well, it ain't only that it's Brandon asking, it's the fact that the gold them outlaws took off with belonged to the Paradise Mine, and there ain't nobody going to turn a hand to help that outfit."

"I heard something about that when I rode up. What's everybody got against the Paradise Mine?"

"They had a chance to set up their office here, and do their buying of supplies from the local merchants. Instead they picked a town on the other side of the

9

mountain. Can't nobody forget that."

Voices in the street rose briefly, fell again to a murmur. Starbuck said, "They probably had a good reason."

"Maybe, but they're going to find out right quick that it'd been smart—and a powerful lot cheaper—to've settled here in Wolf Crossing. . . A hundred thousand dollars cheaper."

Shawn whistled softly. "Lot of money. What happened?"

"They was sending it to Dodge City—some special deal. Usually all the gold goes the other way, to Denver, but this was different, and it was all real secret like. The gold was on two pack mules and they had four guards with them. Was passing themselves off as engineers. Only it didn't work. Somehow the outlaws, was three of them, got wind of the truth about it."

"They pull the holdup here in town?"

"Nope, about a mile east of here. Ambushed them. Brandon heard the shooting, got out there fast as he could, but the outlaws were already gone. One of the guards was still alive, barely. Told the marshal what had happened."

"When was this?"

"Just around noon. Guards had spent the night here, was heading out for Dodge. Brandon brung the bodies in, then sent word to the Paradise people. He's been trying to get a posse together ever since."

Shawn sipped at his whiskey. "Won't the company be sending him some help?"

"Probably, but it'll be this time tomorrow at least before they can get here. Them outlaws will be long gone by then."

The sounds in the street lifted again. Shawn listened

10

idly for a few moments. Harry Brandon, he gathered, was still having no luck.

"Your marshal holds off much more himself, he'll be too late, too. Better settle for those three who did volunteer."

The barman cocked his head to one side, smiled wryly. "If you was him, would you be willing to go after three killers with the town drunk, a greenhorn and a nigra handyman?"

"It'd be a mean choice," Shawn replied, shrugging. "I don't know any of them, but seems they'd be better than nobody at all."

"Doubt that. The greenhorn—name's Walt Moody—blew in here a week or so ago. From St. Louis. Got himself some kind of woman trouble. All he's done is mope around, head hanging and acting like he wish't he was dead. The nigra's been working for some cattle outfit west of here. He got laid off . . . . There's something peculiar about him."

"Peculiar?"

"Well, I mean he's sort of had some learning. Talks real good for a nigra, which is sort of funny."

"A colored man can be educated same as a white. I've known a few in my lifetime."

The bartender nodded. "Sure, I know that, only it sort of surprises a man. You just don't expect it, somehow."

"He got a name?"

"Calls himself Able Rome . . . . Third fellow is Dave Gilder. Lays around here drunk most of the time. Now and then he gets himself a job on some ranch where they don't know him, but it never lasts long. I figure he'd make a pretty good man if he was to get his snout out of the jug and straighten up."

Starbuck finished off the rye, refilled the tumbler with

11

water. The bartender looked at him closely.

"You looking for work? I heard Brandon say he was paying five dollars a day and keep. Good chance the Paradise people will come through with a little reward, too, if they get their hundred thousand back."

Shawn drank the water, shook his head. "No thanks. I got a job of my own to do—looking for my brother."

The man behind the counter paused in the process of wiping the varnished surface of the bar. "He live around here? Maybe I'll know him."

"Name's Ben Starbuck. Good chance he goes by Damon Friend, however."

The bartender resumed his polishing in thoughtful silence. Finally he glanced up. "Nope, don't recollect nobody by either of them names. What's he look like?"

"Probably a little like me. Could be shorter, heavier."

"You talk like you ain't sure—"

"I'm not. Haven't seen him in over ten years or so. Ran off from home after a squabble with my pa."

"I see. . . . You got some reason for thinking he's here in Wolf Crossing?"

"No, I'm just passing through on my way to Santa Fe. I make a point of asking about him wherever I happen to be. Been doing it for a long time—all over the country."

"Must be mighty important that you find him."

"It is. Can't settle Pa's estate until I do . . . . The Grand Central Hotel, that the best place to put up for the night? Been a rough day and I can use a good bed."

"It's the only place, but it's good. Best you do your eating at the Antelope Cafe, howsomever. Vittles are a mite better. How long you aim to be around?"

"Moving on in the morning," Shawn replied. "How much I owe you?"

12

"Two bits'll cover it . . . . You mind me saying something?"

Starbuck dropped a coin on the bar. "Depends."

"About the way you handled them two smart alecks out there in the street. I was standing in the door watching. You—you're powerful fast with that iron of yours."

"A man learns."

"You—maybe, well—could be you sometimes hire out to somebody—"

"If you're wondering if I'm a hired gun, the answers no."

The bartender nodded, looked down. "No offense."

"None taken, and there's times when I have hired on a job where a gun was part of the deal. But only a part."

"I see . . . . This here brother of yours that you're hunting for, if he ever shows up, what ought I to tell him?"

"Could be you won't have to tell him nothing, Ed," a voice said from the doorway. "Could be I know where he is."

Starbuck drew himself upright, wheeled quickly. Harry Brandon, light filtering in from a window glinting against his star, was facing him.

"What was that?"

The lawman came on into the saloon. Beyond him in the street Shawn could see that the crowd had broken up. The three volunteers for the posse now stood at the hitchrack.

"I said I might could tell you where this fellow—"

"Brother—" the bartender supplied.'

This brother of yours, name of Ben, could be."

Starbuck studied the marshal's weathered features narrowly. Then, "Where?"

13

"Like as not he's one of the outlaws I'm setting out after."

CHAPTER 3

STARBUCK'S MOUTH TIGHTENED. EVIDENTLY BRANDON had been standing in the saloon's entrance long enough to overhear part of the conversation he'd had with the Square Dollar's bartender and was trying to make the most of it.

"Not likely," he said coolly.

"Other way about. It's probably true."

"Ben's no outlaw."

"If you ain't seen him in quite a spell, how'd you know for sure?" the lawman said, coming on into the room and taking a place at the bar. "Give me a whiskey, Ed," he said to the aproned man, and then, facing Shawn, added, "He could've changed. Maybe he was all right at the start, but just sort of slid into bad ways."

"No man just gradually turns bad," Starbuck said shrugging. "Somewhere along he gets a chance to say no to something—and Ben's the kind who would have said it."

Harry Brandon stirred indifferently, took up his shot glass of liquor and tossed it off. "Could be you're right. I'm only telling you that one of them killers is named Ben—and if he's the Ben I'm thinking he is, he's about your size and he's got your looks."

A faint smile tugged at Starbuck's lips. He was buying none of it; Harry Brandon was simply trying to recruit a fourth member for his posse. Still. . .

Ed refilled the lawman's glass. "How'd you happen to know one of them was named Ben? You said you

14

didn't see none of them."

"And I didn't. One of them guards wasn't dead, like I told everybody. He recognized a couple of them, give me their names. Ben Snow was one. Another'n was Ollie Kastman. Didn't know the third man. And like I'm saying, if this Ben Snow's the man I've got in mind, he sort of fits the description of your brother."

Starbuck laughed. "Forget it, Marshal. I'm not about to join your posse—if that's what this is all about."

Brandon downed his liquor. "Suit yourself. Ain't saying I wouldn't like to have you with me, but it's up to you."

"You get anybody else, Harry?" the bartender asked.

"Only them three." the lawman replied in a voice filled with disgust. "Don't know what the hell's eating folks around here."

"I expect you do." Ed countered quietly. "If it was anybody but that Paradise outfit, you'd maybe have your posse."

"Maybe."

The saloonman's brows lifted. "Well, you ain't exactly overloaded with friends, Harry."

"No fault of mine. Man wearing a badge has to do his duty. Sometimes tromping on folks' toes can't be helped." The lawman sighed, shoved his glass aside, "Sure is something! It's hell if I do and hell if I don't when it comes to getting my job done."

Two men drifted in through the doorway, sidled up to the bar. Ed moved off to serve their needs. Shawn felt the marshal's hard, dark eyes pressing him.

"I'll ask you straight out—you interested in riding for me? Pay is five dollars a day and grub. Could be an extra hundred or two if the mine comes through with a reward. I expect it won't take more'n three, four

15

days . . . You in a hurry to reach Santa Fe?"

"No."

"I could sure use you—it's the law saying that. Them I got—hell—there ain't the makings of one good man in all three. A sobering-up drunk, a greenhorn and a black boy—might as well go it alone!"

"Sounds like you know where to find the killers."

"I do—pretty well, that is. Guard said they headed south after that ambush. I followed their tracks for a spell. Was easy. Three horses and two mules leave a lot of prints. They circled town, then cut into the mountains."

Shawn had a quick recollection of the sprawling mass of rock and timber towering behind the settlement.

"Won't be easy tracking through—"

"Easier'n you think. My hunch is they're lining out on the trail that goes up to the ridge and cuts clean through the mountains. Old one—Indians used it when they was running wild around here. It's the only way a man can cross over, and there ain't no turning off once you're on it."

"Where'll it take them to?"

"These here mountains run into the Sangre de Cristos, and then they sort of tail off into the Sandias and the Manzanos that run along the east side of the Rio Grande river. They just keep right on going and they'll end up close to the Mexican border. That's where I figure they're headed for—Mexico."

"They got a pretty good start—five, six hours."

"I know that and it's what's got me in a sweat. They're working deeper into them hills every minute and I sure got to be moving out after them. Just one thing good, they won't be traveling fast. Mules'll slow them down plenty."

The bartender returned hurriedly, evidently hopeful of missing nothing. He squinted at Shawn. "You decided to go?"

Starbuck stared at the backbar moodily. Brandon's attempt to interest him by stating that one of the outlaws could be Ben was undoubtedly nothing more than a ruse. The lawman was desperate and willing to try anything . . . . But on the other hand the dying guard had named the outlaws, or two of them, and one he'd said was called Ben.

That much he could probably consider the truth. The remainder—that the man Ben Snow fit the description he'd given of his brother to the bartender—was likely an outright lie on the marshal's part. Trouble was, there was no way of knowing for sure, and he'd made it a rule never to pass up a lead or ignore a possibility that could take him to Ben Starbuck.

Boot heels scraped in the doorway. Shawn glanced up into the mirror, saw Brandon turn. Able Rome hesitated just within the batwings, then moved toward the bar.

"All right, boy," the lawman said impatiently. "I'm coming. You and the others get your horses, meet me at the stable."

Rome did not slow his steps, continued until he reached the long counter. "I'm ready when you are, Marshal," he said in a soft, slurred accent. "Whiskey," he added, nodding to the bartender.

Ed reached for a glass, filled it and slid it along the counter. Brandon frowned.

"You do much drinking, boy?"

Rome's expression did not alter. "No more than the next man, I expect."

"Well, I want you to get this straight right now, I won't stand for no drinking on this hunt!"

17

"What I carry will be in my belly," Rome replied and downed his whiskey. He reached into his pocket, produced a quarter and laid it on the counter. Wheeling, he crossed to the doors and returned to the street.

"Uppity cuss," Brandon murmured, watching until the man had disappeared. "Ain't so sure I want him coming along, only I reckon I can't be choicey." He swung his attention to Shawn.

"What about it? I ain't saying Ben Snow is your brother, but I am saying there's a mighty good chance he is. Riding with me is one way you can find out."

Starbuck gave it another moment's thought, shrugged. "All right, I'll go. I'm not believing anything you say about it being my brother, but I'm willing to have myself proved wrong."

"Good," Brandon said, smiling broadly. "Just might find yourself surprised. We'll be moving out right away."

"Going to take me a few minutes. I got to get myself a fresh horse. Sorrel of mine's had a hard day. I need to buy a new canteen—"

"Forget it. I've got an extra you can have. And far as changing horses is concerned, you won't have to. Figure to make camp at Gold Creek—about ten miles back in the mountains. That animal of yours can make it that far."

"I expect I'm ready then," Shawn said, and nodding to the bartender, turned for the door.

CHAPTER 4

THEY RODE OUT OF WOLF CROSSING WITH THE DARK clouds still clinging to the mountain peaks, seemingly poised and awaiting only the proper moment to open their overloaded bellies and send a flood cascading down the long slopes.

Shawn, though feeling hunger, had passed up the few minutes of grace permitted him while Harry Brandon made his final preparations—time during which he could have grabbed a hasty bite at the restaurant mentioned by Ed, the bartender—and instead made use of them to water the sorrel and see to his gear.

The marshal had said they would travel only a short distance before making camp; he could ignore his need for food until then—and the sorrel was a different matter. He had gone the entire day without water.

Riding beside Brandon, Starbuck glanced back as they broke clear of the town's limits and turned off the well-defined road toward the towering mountains. Behind the lawman and him came Moody and Dave Gilder, their horses side by side and matching each step. Able Rome, his broad face emotionless, brought up the rear. He had not spoken, so far as Shawn know, since he had been in the saloon.

"Mighty glad you showed up when you did," Brandon said, shifting his holster forward on his leg. "I figured I had to have at least one good man along that I could depend on—and you was him."

Starbuck half smiled. "You don't know me, Marshal. How can you say that?"

"Shows—that's how. I'm a pretty good judge of men, and on you it shows."

"Plain guess. Doubt if I'm any more reliable than the men you've got."

The lawman snorted. "You talking about Gilder and Moody and that nigra?"

"I'm talking about Gilder and Moody and Able Rome," Starbuck said coldly.

19

Brandon turned his head, considered Shawn for a long breath. "Yeh, them. Like I said, they don't count for hardly nothing. Just three bags of corn husks setting on three saddles." He paused, swept the riders behind him with a scornful glance. "Brandon's posse—hell! Best you call them Brandon's misfits."

"Could be wrong about them."

"Wrong—how?"

"All most men need sometimes is a chance, one that'll make them face up to something hard and force them to prove themselves. Somebody once said that a hero was never born, he was made."

"Not them! What can Dave Gilder prove to himself? He can't even keep hisself sober long enough to do much of anything. And about all the proving he could do me is that he could go a whole day without a drink, which I sure doubt.

"And that greenhorn—Moody. What's he got to prove? That he ain't already dead from something that happened to him sometime or other? He's done showed that he wasn't man enough to take it—else he wouldn't be nothing but a walking corpse."

"Hard to know what's in any man's mind."

"Not with them it ain't. Gilder's figuring how soon it'll be before he can get back to town and blow what money he'll make on whiskey. Moody's trying to forget whatever it is that's chewing on his guts, and far as that nig—that Rome's concerned, he's just out to show he's good as any white man. Always the way with them black ones."

Harry Brandon spat, looked ahead. The trail was slipping down into the bottom of a fairly narrow canyon to pick its course along the floor. Pine trees were beginning to be more plentiful, and the lesser growth common to the lower valley and flats area was thinning out.

"They might as well try changing their color," the lawman said, resuming the subject. "That's what's eating them." He frowned, fixed Shawn with his hard, fixed gaze. "You got a special feeling for blacks?"

"I never thought about it one way or another. Just a man like any other—"

"Then you sure'n hell ain't never had much truck with them!"

"I've worked with a few, and we had a couple of hired hands back on the farm that were colored. Never figured them as being anything other than two men who worked for my pa."

"Where was that?"

"Ohio. Place was on the Muskingum River. Town nearby had the same name."

"Ohio," Brandon repeated as if it explained much to him. "Your people still there?"

"No. My mother's been dead a long time—about twelve years now. Pa died two years ago."

"And that's what cut you loose and started you hunting this brother you was talking about."

Starbuck nodded. "I've been at it off an' on ever since. I have to stop once in awhile, find myself a job and get a little traveling money together."

"I come from a farm myself," the lawman said in a thoughtful voice. "Pennsylvania. Wish't the hell I'd a stayed there. Good land, good house and not no worrying to do like I've had since I got out here."

"You always worn a badge?"

"Yep, first job I took was being a deputy sheriff. Up in Colorado. Had a couple others like it—Wyoming, Nebraska, then I got myself elected marshal of this

21

damned hole. . . . Been sorry of it."

Shawn glanced up, surprised. "I understood from that bartender—"

"Ed Christian—"

"Whatever his name is, that you were up for re-election next month."

"He say that?"

"Not in so many words but it's the way I took it."

Brandon laughed. "Yeh, I reckon he'd be thinking that. He's one of the town councilmen—him and Gooch and Stratton and Doc Marberry—and they'd be figuring on me going after the job again. But they got a big surprise coming. They can take the job and shove it because I'm pulling out. Had all of that town I want."

There was a bitterness in the lawman's tone and his features had become grim.

"How long you been wearing the badge in Wolf Crossing?"

"Six years—almost, and that's more'n enough. No help there when you need it, nobody ever willing to back you up. This posse's a good example of how they feel about the law—me. . . . I need support, ask for it and what do I get? Them!" Brandon finished with a sweeping gesture toward the men behind him.

"I expect the fact that it was the Paradise Mine people they'd be helping was the big reason."

The marshal shook his head, spat. "Nah, the mining company is just something to lay it on. Me—I'm the one they're turning their backs on. But I don't give a good goddam no more. Hell of a life, anyway. No future in it. A man gets too old to work, he gets let out, ends up swamping in a saloon or forking manure in a stable. . . . Pay's never enough for him to lay any money aside.

22

"But I'm beating them at their own game. No little two-bit town's going to do that to me. I'm quitting, getting out while the getting's good. Already made my plans."

"If that's the way you feel about it," Shawn said, "then that's the thing to do. A man only lives once. I reckon he ought to fill his time doing what he likes."

"That's me exactly, from here on," Brandon replied. "Leastwise it'll be after I hand in my star."

Starbuck made no comment. Darkness was growing and he began to look ahead for signs of. the creek where they would be making night camp. He'd be glad to crawl off the saddle and have a meal. It had been a long, tiring day.

Brandon, noting his exploring glance, said, "We'll be pulling up in another mile or so. Gold Creek ain't far. . . . I hear you say you was headed for Santa Fe?"

Shawn nodded. He was a bit weary of conversation, hoped the lawman had talked himself out for awhile but evidently it was not to be.

"Somebody there you know—or maybe you're just hoping to find your brother?"

"I aim to look for him, do some asking around."

"I expect you've seen a passel of places, drifting around the way you have."

"Quite a few, all right."

"Country south of the mountains—the range we're following—you been there?"

"Not too much. Worked around Las Cruces for a time."

"Where's that?"

"Lower Rio Grande Valley. . . .Some call it the Mesilla Valley."

"Ain't that pretty close to the Mexican border?"

"Forty, fifty miles, as I recall."

Off to their right a piñon jay scolded noisily from the depths of a long-needled pine. Brandon listened briefly and then said, "What's back up this side of Las Cruces?"

"A lot of open country—desert, unless you stay down in the valley where the Rio Grande is."

"But east of that, there ain't much of nothing, that it?"

"About right. A few lonesome hills, and a man can run into Indians if he's not watching sharp. Apaches and Comanches both."

"But a man could get through if he was well fixed for grub and water and kept his eyes peeled."

Brandon was evidently thinking about the outlaws they were pursuing, the possibility of their escaping to make their way to the Mexican border.

"That's what they'll need—along with some good luck."

"Which they sure'n hell ain't going to get the chance of using!" the lawman said harshly.

Starbuck's gaze rested on Harry Brandon. There was solid, cold determination in his tone and manner. Overtaking the killers and recovering the gold apparently was very important to him. He guessed he could understand the lawman's thinking; he was turning in his star and he wanted to do it with success crowning the moment.

Perhaps he even hoped the people of Wolf Crossing would suddenly realize their loss and beg him to stay; then he could laugh in their faces and turn them down cold.

"Reckon we're here—"

The marshal's voice brought Shawn's attention to the trail. A dozen strides ahead he saw a narrow ribbon of

24

water sparkling dully in the fading daylight as it cut its way along the foot of a slope. He heaved a deep sigh. A hot meal was going to do him a lot of good.

Dave Gilder cupped his hands over the saddlehorn and allowed his suffering body to rock back and forth with the motion of his horse. Every nerve within his being was crying that all too familiar cry.

He had known it was coming, that the craving would hit him hardest on the third day—and this was the third day, or rather the evening of the third. But this time he was going to lick it. He'd tipped his last bottle and from now on he was going to be master of his own self.

High time, he thought bitterly. He should have done it years ago. If he had, it would be an entirely different sort of life he'd be leading. Likely he'd be in business somewhere, or maybe he would have had himself a ranch or a farm. Hell, he had plenty of ability—he'd proved that during the war when he headed up the quartermaster department of the corps he was in.

But most of all he'd still have Felicity and the three boys. They'd all be together, living and growing as a family should. . . . He reckoned he could forget all that—them. He didn't even blame Felicity anymore for taking the boys and leaving him and going home to her folks in Georgia. He hadn't been a husband or a father, he'd been nothing but a worthless drunk.

Maybe—just maybe, mind you—if he could straighten up this time and stay that way. Felicity would come back. Oh, sure, he'd tried it before, but something always came up to change things and before he knew what was happening, he found himself sprawled in the back room of some saloon or in a flophouse of a hotel sleeping off a three- or four-day bout with old John

25

Barleycorn.

But this time it was different. He had a feeling about it. He'd not slip, he'd stay cold, stone sober and not even think about a drink . . . . Three days now, and while all hell was breaking loose inside him, he'd fight it out to a finish. This time he'd beat it—win.

Walt Moody slid a glance at the, man riding beside him. The marshal had evidently just said something about them to that gunslinger he'd talked into becoming a member of his posse, and he wondered if the fellow had noticed. It hadn't been complimentary, that was for sure. The look on the lawman's face had proved that.

Not that it mattered. Nothing did anymore, although he had tried often enough to pick up the bits and pieces of his life and fit them back together into a satisfactory whole. Perhaps he would be better off if he were like Gilder and could submerge his memories and thoughts and lost hopes in a bottle of whiskey. But liquor had never been of any help; indeed, it had only made matters worse.

It did something to his mind, brought into sharp focus all the plans he'd once entertained and the dreams he had sought to convert into reality. But worst of all it called forth from the dark, shadowy comers of his brain a graphic remembrance, a vivid portrait of Rozella in all her haunting, ethereal beauty to stand before him like a vengeful, accusing ghost.

It never entirely faded, simply receded leaving him always aware of its lurking, destroying presence. He didn't know what the answer to his life would be, and for a year now he'd been searching for it. Somewhere there was a solution, a relief from the past and thoughts of all the things that could have been but were not.

26

Perhaps he would find it on this manhunt; maybe it lay in danger, in the hammer of gunshots, the whir of bullets—the sight of blood. He had looked everywhere else and found nothing. Could it be that death was the key—the final vindication? If so, and the espousers of religion were right, he'd be with Rozella again.

Able Rome considered the heavy clouds hanging low in the already dark sky. It was going to rain, no doubt of it. Maybe not that very night but it would come before sundown tomorrow. A hard rain would make him feel good. It always did. It gave him a sort of cleaned-off, scoured sensation like when, as a boy, his ma had worked him over in a tubful of suds with a stiff bristled brush.

A storm could complicate the marshal's plans to track down those outlaws and the gold they were running with, however. That was good, too; he was drawing five big dollars for every day he put in with the posse. There could be a little something extra, too, the marshal had said, if they recovered the gold for the mining company.

He could use a couple of hundred dollars. It would give his poke a real boost and put him that much closer to owning that place down in Arizona he planned to have. But he still had a long way to go before he'd be in shape to settle down. Money wasn't easy to come by. He was always the first to be laid off a job, the last to be hired—not because he wasn't a good cowhand; he knew he was better and more reliable than most, but a black man always had to take the leavings.

His pa had been wrong there, even if he had been plenty smart in almost everything else. The personal bodyservant of a New Orleans plantation owner, he had been tutored privately and had learned to read and write—even think—like a white man.

He had passed on his learning to Able, assuring him all the while that education and knowledge was the open door to things, that by possessing it he would be the equal of any man regardless of where he went. *It's being ignorant that makes the difference*, he had said.

But Able had found it to be untrue. In fact, it seemingly had just the opposite effect; those of his own kind shunned him, called him *high-toned*, and as for the whites, they either ignored him or were suspicious and hated him.

During the war when he had served with the Union Army he had attempted to make use of his abilities for the good of the Cause but his superiors had been uninterested and he had stayed in the ranks along with others of his color, doing the same menial tasks assigned to those with no education at all.

That was when it began to dawn on him that his father had been wrong; there was more to it than being able to read and write and talk intelligently. Somewhere along the way you had to reach a different level of proof as to a man being a man.

The burgeoning West offered possibilities where it could be attained, and when the fighting was over he had taken the money he'd managed to accumulate, bought himself a horse and gear, and headed for Texas and points farther on.

Now, eleven years later, he was still searching for that level of proof, that elusive something that would provide him with the means by which he could take his rightful place and be accepted and equal to all those with whom he came in contact.

It shouldn't really be so important to him anymore, he often told himself; he was doing pretty good, actually

28

far better than most of his kind. He had money saved, plans for a small ranch of his own, and while he was relegated to that airless, lonely chasm lying between the black people and the white—a limbo where he was neither fish nor fowl—he reckoned he should not complain.

But it troubled Able Rome nevertheless. Just what was it he must do to attain that intangible factor Mr. Lincoln had called equality? Just as all journeys must begin with a first step, he had begun at the knee of his father; after that it had all seemed to stall and the goal he sought receded farther into the gloomy distance.

He shrugged. It was a thing to puzzle a man, and he for one would like to find the answer. . . . Not that it really mattered. . . . A wry smile tugged at his lips as the old, familiar rationalization slipped effortlessly into his mind. The hell it didn't matter! It mattered a lot. The five dollars a day he was to get as a posse member wasn't important at all—it was the chance to prove that he was a man—a damn good man equal to any that walked the earth with him and not just another black—a nigger—with a bit of education.

CHAPTER 4

THEY RODE INTO A SMALL CLEARING THAT PARALLELED the stream, and dismounted.

"All right, boy," Brandon said, crooking a finger at Rome. "I'm appointing you the hostler for this outfit. Look after the horses."

Able Rome, blandly ignoring the lawman's words, turned, began to loosen his saddle cinch. Back up the slope in the darkening trees an owl hooted.

"You hear me?"

Starbuck faced the marshal. "He's got a name. Might try using it," he drawled.

Brandon gave Shawn a contemptuous side glance, spat, bobbed his head. "Why, sure . . . Mister Rome." he said with exaggerated politeness, "I'll be obliged to you for looking after the horses."

Able smiled faintly, began to gather up the trailing reins of the five mounts.

"And you two—Mister Gilder and Mister Moody, start dragging in some wood for a fire," the lawman continued. He swung his sardonic gaze to Shawn. "If you don't mind, Mister Starbuck, youll do the cooking."

Shawn nodded coolly to the marshal, neither angered nor amused by his broad irony.

"Sack of grub hanging on my saddle. Go light on it. Liable to have to last a few days," Brandon said and, moving to where Rome was picketing the horses, drew the rifle from his saddle boot.

"Taking me a look up the trail. Back in a few minutes."

Starbuck watched him stride off and then crossed to get the flour sack of supplies hanging from Brandon's saddle. As he pulled at the cord securing it, he felt Rome's eyes upon him and looked up. The man's features were taut.

"Don't go out of your way to do me any favors," he said in a low voice. "I can look after myself."

"I expect you can," Shawn replied indifferently. "It wasn't meant as a favor."

"I've been bucking up against men like the marshal all my life and I've got my own way of handling them. I don't need you or anybody else horning in for me just because I'm colored."

30

Rome's words did bespeak some measure of education, Shawn realized, but his belligerent attitude more than offset the asset.

"That wasn't the reason for it," he said and, wheeling, returned to the center of the clearing where Dave Gilder, sweat standing out on his forehead in large beads despite the coolness, was placing stones in the customary horseshoe arrangement.

"I expect the marshal'll want the fire kept low," he said. "He won't want to let them outlaws know we're on their heels."

Starbuck agreed, began to dig around in the sack of grub. Brandon had neglected to bring a large spider or a coffee pot of suitable size, forcing him to fall back on his own trail equipment. Again he was conscious of Able Rome's dark-eyed consideration as he probed his own saddlebags for the necessary items, but the man said nothing and he had no words for him.

A time later Harry Brandon returned, The meal of fried meat, potatoes, warmed-over bread and coffee was under way on the fire. Gilder and Moody, their supply of wood gathered and nearby, had brought in the blanket rolls and placed them about where they would be handy. Able Rome, his charges watered and now grazing on plentiful grass, hunkered in solitary silence at the edge of the glow.

"Ahead of us, just like I knowed they'd be," the lawman said, propping his rifle against a tree. "That grub about ready?"

"About," Starbuck answered. We moving after them tonight?"

Brandon glanced about the camp, giving it his appraisal. "No hurry—and no point. They can't give us the slip now, there being only one trail. . . . Be a mite

31

risky in the dark, anyway."

Shawn let it drop. It was up to the lawman and he evidently didn't feel it was necessary to close in at once. Besides, the long hours he had already put in on the sorrel were beginning to catch up to him.

Thunder growled in the distance. Brandon glanced at the black sky, murmured, "Reckon it's a-coming," and walked to where Rome had fitted his saddle over a clump of mountain mahogany. Pulling at the tie strings behind the cantle, he freed his brush jacket and pulled it on.

Settling it about his torso, he reached into an inner pocket and produced a pint bottle of whiskey. Making no effort to conceal his actions, he drew the cork and treated himself to a healthy swallow. Then, smacking his lips and brushing his mustache, he replaced the cork in the container and returned it to his pocket, seemingly oblivious of the watching men.

"Grub's ready," Starbuck said, glancing at Dave Gilder.

The shine of sweat was again on his haggard face as he stared into the fire. Raising a hand, he ran his fingers unsteadily through his thinning red hair.

Able Rome, plate in hand, came forward at once, began to help himself from the contents of the two spiders. Brandon, unsmiling, waited until the black man had finished and then took his turn, plainly irritated. Gilder followed and Shawn then looked expectantly at Moody, who had not stirred.

"You're next."

The immobile, sallow features of the man altered slightly. He shrugged half-heartedly, took up a plate and portioned out a small amount of the food. Shawn gave him a questioning smile.

"Either you don't have much of an appetite or my cooking's not as good as I figured."

"Foods fine—just not hungry," Moody said in an apologetic tone. "Coffee's what I need most."

Starbuck pushed one of the containers at the man and turned to fill his own plate. He hadn't eaten since breakfast—and then but little—and hunger was pushing at him.

They ate in silence, all but Walt Moody wolfing down the food, and when it was gone made their way to the creek, where each cleaned his plate and tools. Shawn made more coffee and after storing the remainder of the supplies where mice and other small animals could not get to them, moved back to the fire and settled down on his folded blanket.

The others were there before him, sprawled in the warm glow. Gilder had produced a pipe, was puffing at it nervously. Both Rome and Moody had built cigarettes, and Shawn dug into his shirt pocket for his sack of tobacco and papers.

"Ought to have a better fire than that," Brandon said cheerfully. Gathering up an armload of dry limbs, he dropped them onto the low flames. "We running short on wood or something?"

Gilder glanced up at the lawman. "I figured you wouldn't want them outlaws to spot us."

The lawman dismissed the thought with a motion of his hand. "Makes no difference. They know—and there ain't nothing they can do about it."

"Except move on," Starbuck said, finishing his smoke and hanging it in a corner of his mouth.

"Not them—not while it's night. They've got two pack mules they won't chance losing. Be daylight before they'll pull out. . . . That there fancy belt you're wearing, does it mean you're a champion fighter or something?"

"No," Shawn replied, looking down at the silver buckle with its superimposed ivory figure of a boxer. "It belonged to my Pa. It was given him by some folks back where I came from. He was good at boxing, but he wasn't a champion. Could have been, I expect, if he wanted."

"You know how to do that kind of fighting?" Gilder asked.

"Pa taught my brother and me—both."

Able Rome flipped his spent cigarette into the surging flames. "I once saw a boxing match," he said, speaking for the first time since words had passed between him and Shawn at their arrival. "It was quite a show."

Starbuck turned to the man. "Was that somewhere around here?"

"No, it was during the war. At the camp where I was stationed."

Shawn settled back. "I thought maybe one of the boxers might've been my brother. He puts on exhibition matches now and then. . . . About the only way I ever turn up a line on him."

"Is he lost or something?" Gilder asked.

"Not lost," Brandon explained. "Starbuck just can't locate him. Been hunting him all over the country for years. He thinks maybe one of them outlaws could be him."

"It was your idea, not mine," Shawn said drily. "But I'm not saying you couldn't be right. It's been a long time since I last saw Ben. He could've changed. I doubt he'd turn to killing as a way of making a living, though."

There was silence after that, broken only by the noisy

34

clacking of innumerable rain crickets filling the night with their prophecies. Able Rome began to roll a fresh cigarette.

"What's he look like? Could be I've run into him somewheres."

Shawn went into details, such as they were, of Ben, noting that he could be living under the name of Damon Friend. When he had finished the men all shook their heads. None could recall ever encountering anyone of either name or who fit the meager description he could supply.

"What's got you figuring he might be one of them killers?" Dave Gilder asked.

Shawn ducked his head at the lawman. "The marshal said one of them is named Ben and that he sort of fills the bill."

Brandon nodded. "If it's the Ben Snow I'm thinking of," he said, tossing more wood into the fire, "he does. You got to remember, howsomever, I ain't seen none of them killers. I only know what the guard told me."

Able Rome studied Starbuck with narrowed eyes. "You volunteer for this posse on the strength of that?"

"Partly. Sometimes I have to go on what I can get— even if it is a slim lead. Otherwise it could turn out someday that I spent a lot of time looking without really looking at all."

"I know what you mean," Dave Gilder murmured, staring into the flames. "A man can keep promising himself tomorrows—that he's going to do something, I mean, and then one day he wakes up and finds out all he's got is a lot of empty yesterdays laying behind him, and he ain't done nothing."

"Just the way it can turn out," Brandon said. Picking up a small clod of dirt, he tossed it at Walt Moody.

35

"Ain't that what you say, greenhorn?"

Moody, in brooding silence through it all, roused himself. Hunched forward, shoulders slumped, he locked his hands together and stared off into the night.

"I don't think I'm an authority on much of anything," he said. "I figure that what's going to happen to a man is going to happen. God's will, I guess you'd call it—"

"God," Gilder broke in, stirring restlessly, "I don't know whether there's such a thing as God or not, but there sure is a hell! I've been in it from the day I was born, and I don't figure I'll be out of it until I'm dead—if then."

Walt Moody shifted his sick eyes to Dave. "I agree with that. The drawback is that a man gets born whether he wants to be or not. Has no say in it—just has to start living and making the best of what comes his way and whatever happens to him. Some make a go of it, others fail—even though they try."

Thunder rolled menacingly again, now somewhat louder and nearer. Brandon grinned across the flickering flames at Able.

"Ain't you got nothing to say about this, Mister Rome? I figured you'd be a genuine humdinger of expert when it comes to this here moaning and groaning about living."

"I expect I am, Marshal," Rome replied coolly, and glanced at Starbuck. "That name of yours—Shawn. Are you part Indian?"

"No. My mother once taught some Shawnee kids. I guess she liked the sound of the word, made it into a name for me."

The answer seemed to disappoint Able Rome. It was as if he had been hoping for a kindred soul in variance. He shrugged, and once again drew out his cigarette makings.

Brandon looked up into the blackness that was the sky, as a deep rumbling was again heard. "Aim to start early in the morning. Reckon we'd best be turning in. Boy—uh, Mister Rome, you sure them horses can't get loose?"

"They'll be there when we want them," Able said.

"Well, they sure better be or—"

Brandon's words were checked as the fire exploded suddenly into a shower of sparks and ashes and burning brands. A split second later, the hollow crack of a gunshot echoed through the night. For a long breath no one moved, and then Starbuck threw himself to one side, clear of the flames' pale glow.

"Get out of the light!" he yelled.

The outlaws had spotted them.

CHAPTER 6

"THAT GODDAM FIRE—" GILDER MUTTERED, PLUNGING backwards into the brush. "Was too big—I knew it!

Shawn, deep in the shadows, leaped to his feet Drawing his pistol, he spun, started up the, trail at a fast run. He heard the thud of boot heels close behind, looked around, expecting Harry Brandon. It was Able Rome.

Together they rushed on, holding to the edge of the path where brush and trees could mask their movements. Back in the direction of the camp Brandon's voice was booming into the night but the loud rasp of their own labored breathing, and the noise of their passage as they raced up the steep grade, made his words unintelligible.

The trail cut right, topped out a small ridge. Starbuck halted, eyes searching the blackness ahead, ears straining to pick up any sound that would reveal the location of the outlaws.

Rome moved up to his side. "Anything?"

Shawn wagged his head.

Able waited until a roll of thunder had died, then said, "Probably gone by now. Saw they'd missed the marshal, or whoever they were shooting at, and run for it."

"About the way of it, but we'll wait a bit," Shawn said, and moving to a log beside the trail, sat down. He sucked in a deep breath, exhaled. "That was a hard climb."

"For a fact," Rome said, finding himself a place on the fallen tree. "What happened to Brandon?"

"Don't know. I heard him yelling, but couldn't get what he was saying."

"Something about coming back."

Starbuck rubbed at his jaw. "I figured he'd be right with us."

"Same here, but I reckon he believes in playing it safe."

Shawn gave that brief thought. "Could be, but Brandon strikes me as a man who's not scared of anything much."

Able Rome was silent for a long moment. Then, "I expected you'd say that," he said in a stiff voice. "The flawless white man, as my pa used to put it."

"Not necessarily," Starbuck came back quickly. "Just stands to reason—and don't go blaming me because you're black and I'm white. I had nothing to do with it and sure as hell can't do anything about it, so, far as I'm concerned, either take that chip off your shoulder or head on back to camp."

38

Far to the west lightning winked across the sky, underscored its presence with a deep rumbling. Able Rome shifted on the log, toyed with the pistol in his hands.

"Is that the way it strikes you—that I'm blaming white men because I'm black?"

Starbuck shrugged. "It's pretty plain to me. Probably looks that way to others."

"That's not it at all," Rome said. "Leastwise, it's not how I feel. . . . I guess it could seem like it." He sighed, holstered his weapon. "All I'm hunting for is the chance to be the same as other men—their equal and not something separate that is to be treated different."

"You've had some education. You ought to realize that the day when that'll come to pass is probably a long time off despite what the war did for your people. This is a white man's country—it was founded by whites and has always been run by whites. It'll be quite a few years before you'll see any change from that, I think."

"That's nothing but prejudice and—?"

"No prejudice to it, just a fact of life. But I won't argue with you about it because that's what you're looking for and arguing won't change anything."

"Maybe you won't because you know I'm right."

"Right—about what?"

"The unfairness of it all."

Starbuck sighed heavily. He'd been caught up in similar word exchanges before, and he knew such conversations accomplished no purpose.

"Nothing unfair to it far as I can see. Maybe the day will come when there'll be no difference in color noticed, but it'll be a while."

"There's no reason why it shouldn't be now. Mr. Lincoln made it plain that it was what he wanted—and why he was fighting a war."

"The purpose of the war was to keep the Union from breaking up. The slavery issue was only part of it."

Rome paused, nodded. "Anyway, he won the war and made it clear that he wanted folks to forget there was a difference in races and—"

"I wasn't in the war myself and maybe you know more about it than I, but the way I understood it was that he made it plain there was to be no more slavery. I think he figured time would take care of the rest."

"That's not the way I took it. I heard him talk once. He came to the camp where I was. He said every man was equal and that it had to be that way."

"I doubt if he meant it exactly like you took it. Sure, all men are born free and equal, but it's up to them from then on. They can do something with their lives or they can waste them."

"And if they never get a chance—"

"Most men do. Some get fewer and perhaps smaller chances than others but they get them. . . . And doing something with a small opportunity usually leads up to a bigger one."

"Not for the blacks."

"For everybody," Starbuck said patiently. "You're a good example—but you're so close to it You can't see it. I—"

Shawn came to his feet slowly. A faint noise up the trail had caught his attention. Hand resting on the butt of his pistol, he stood motionless in the darkness listening into the night. The sound did not come again, and after a bit he settled back on the log. Some small animal rustling about in the dry leaves, he supposed.

He was rested now from the hurried climb he had made and his breathing was again at normal flow. The thought of his blanket back at camp, and a few hours of sleep, brought him to his feet again.

"I expect we'd best be heading down-trail," he said.

Rome drew himself upright. "You said I was a good example. . . . Example of what?"

"What a man can do to pull himself up to a higher notch."

"I was luckier than most blacks. My father got some schooling."

"How?"

"Man who owned him gave it to him."

"Why?"

Able Rome's head came up. "Why? Because he wanted him to have it, I reckon."

"Exactly. He wanted him to have some education and helped him to get it. It wasn't because he was black or because he felt sorry for him. It was because he wanted him to have it. Chances are he would, or maybe did, do as much for some white man. There're plenty of them, too, you know, who can't read or write and have never been able to get anywhere in this life. . . . Colored people don't have a patent on being poor and having things hard."

Starbuck, warming slightly under the discussion, moved out onto the trail and started slowly down the grade. Rome, thoughtful for several moments, quickly caught up with him.

"I hadn't looked at it that way, and I expect it's true, but it's the white who always get help first. They're favored when it comes to jobs, things like that—and you can't tell me it's not so."

"I won't even try. I'll tell you this much, I've been to a lot of places, seen a lot of things, and there's plenty of men who hire on the strength of ability—not color. I won't say it happens every time, because it doesn't, but

41

it's sure not as bad as you seem to think."

"Then why does it happen I'm the one that's let off a job first, and always find it hard to get back on?"

"Could be that chip on your shoulder," Starbuck said dryly. "It's a foot wide and a yard long. . . . You—yourself—forget about being colored. Don't even think about it and most everybody you come up against will forget it, too. Quit trying so hard to be a man—and just be one. The way you're going about it now the hate's sticking out all over you."

"It'd be a waste of time. Men like Brandon—"

"There'll always be his kind, and it's not only colored people they take their bigotry out on. Count in the Chinese, the Indians, Mexicans, Italians, Spaniards, all races that aren't the same as they are."

"I know that but—"

"And we're not all that way. You'll find several rotten potatoes in a sackful. You believe that every colored man is good and honest and fair?"

"No, of course not."

"It works the same with white people. We've plenty of the kind we're not proud of and it's wrong to judge the whole by the few. Now, I expect you'd find most men would treat you all right if you'd give them a chance, but that cloud of hate you're wearing like a halo won't even let them get close."

Able Rome swore quietly, helplessly "That's been the only defense I've had—only thing I could do. Other way got me nowhere."

"Maybe. You can't be sure. The big thing you've got to remember is that you're not going to change it a overnight It'll take time—and that's another fact of life."

Rome's shoulders lifted, fell. "Maybe I'm beginning

to see. . . . My pa once told me something I never did for sure understand. He said the weather won't wear a sharp rock smooth in just a day or even a year—that it sometimes took a lifetime. . . . I think now I know what he was driving at."

"He must have been a wise man."

"He was. I think about him in the same light as I think about Mr. Lincoln. He had a deep-down way of looking at things and making sense of them. I wish they could have met and talked.

"I keep remembering things they both said, but I think I remember most what Mr. Lincoln told us once about ideas. He said that once a man had one and got it stuck in his mind, there was nothing anybody could do about taking it away from him. And if he told his idea to others and it was a good one, it'd stay in their minds, too, and keep on growing even though the man who started it was dead and gone.

"That's how I think about myself and other Negroes. We're free and we're good as anybody else. The same God lives in us that lives in white people and we're entitled to walk shoulder to shoulder with every other living person and not always be apologizing for what we are. . . . They killed Mr. Lincoln for thinking that— starting the idea."

"They?"

"Some say it was the people close to him, the politicians. Others claim it was a bunch of Confederates, crazy mad because they lost the war. I reckon nobody really knows for certain—but in the end it didn't make any difference. They couldn't kill and bury the idea he started and I expect that's what counts—the good things a man leaves behind after he's gone.

"Anyway, it's what I live by—that idea. All I want to

do is prove I'm a man, not a Negro, or a nigger, or a black—but a man."

"Starbuck!" Harry Brandon's shout came from down the trail. "That you?"

"Right," Shawn yelled back.

Able Rome laughed in a quiet, desperate sort of way.

"You see? I'm not even here—don't exist. He knew we both went up that trail, but he called out your name—not mine. He didn't even yell for us both—only you. How do I prove that I'm alive?"

CHAPTER 7

ONLY A FEW FAINTLY GLOWING EMBERS. REMAINED OF the bullet-shattered fire as Shawn and Able Rome rounded the last clump of brush and stepped into the clearing. At once Harry Brandon, bristling with anger, strode toward them.

"What the hell you mean taking off like that?"

Starbuck pulled up in surprise. "I thought we were here to catch those outlaws."

"We are, but by God, we're doing it my way!"

Shawn stirred wearily. "What difference does it make whose way it is as long as we get them? Whoever fired that shot wasn't far up the trail. Could be, if we'd all gone after him, we might've finished this job tonight."

"And maybe we could've got ourselves filled full of lead, too, tearing around in the dark like that!" the lawman snapped.

Shawn wagged his head, glanced at Dave Gilder. The man's features were bleak, hungering, and his eyes were fixed on the bulge the bottle of whiskey made in Brandon's pocket. Moody, apparently half asleep,

44

slumped against a stump and was taking no interest in any of it.

"I doubt if they could see any farther in the dark than we could."

"I ain't saying they could, but they sure'n hell knew you was coming up the trail. Likely just set there and watched. . . . Goddam lucky you're alive. Now, from here on, you wait for me to give you orders, understand?"

"Whatever you say, Marshal," Starbuck replied indifferently.

He looked at Able Rome, who had stood to one side listening quietly but was now moving off toward the horses. Brandon had ignored him throughout the tongue-lashing, and directed his anger at Shawn alone. It was as if he felt he could expect nothing different from Rome and thereby excused his actions, but Starbuck, being a white man, should have known better. More fuel for the smoldering fires of outrage that glowed in Able Rome's breast, Starbuck thought tiredly.

A bright streak of lightning flooded the clearing. Thunder rolled ominously. Brandon glanced about, said: "Going to get plenty wet before morning. Best you all get yourself set for it."

There was little they could do. None of them had brought a tarp, only blankets which were useless when it came to shedding rain. Shawn had his slicker, and recalled he'd seen like gear on the saddles of Brandon and Rome. If a downpour set in he could share his with Moody, using it as a canopy. It would be up to one of the others to do the same with Dave Gilder.

He gave that some thought as he set about collecting a supply of wood for the morning cookfire and storing it back under the brush where it could remain dry. If that

45

came to pass it would be interesting to see which of the two made the offer—Brandon or Rome.

The night was once again filled with a blinding flash of palest blue. Almost immediately thunder set up its rolling echoes. Shawn paused, swung his attention to Dave Gilder spreading his blanket on the opposite side of the clearing.

"Close," he said.

Gilder only nodded, continuing to prepare his bed.

Starbuck, satisfied that he had sufficient wood cached, moved to where his saddle lay, and picking it up, carried it back to his blanket roll which had been placed next to Walt Moody's. Pulling his slicker free, he shook it out, laid it close by where it would be handy, and then settled down.

Harry Brandon stood at the edge of the camp staring off into the blackness of the slope. He could be wondering if the outlaws posed a threat for the night, Shawn guessed, and he could also be realizing that it might have been better for the entire posse to have gone in search of the rifleman who had scattered the fire—and who probably wasn't alone.

But if that was his thought, the lawman would never admit it. He was not the kind to acknowledge a mistake—that had become apparent earlier.

"You see anything up there?" Moody asked as he began to draw his blanket about him.

"No, we didn't," Starbuck replied, making a point of the pronoun. There was some justification for Rome's attitude.

"We wanted to follow. The marshal said no—was too big a risk to take."

"Not much difference in staying here and maybe getting picked off one by one."

46

"I suppose not," Moody said heavily. "I don't think we're going to get much sleep—especially if it starts raining."

"You can figure on it," Shawn said, "but it could hold off until morning." He paused, looked more closely at Moody's pale features, oddly lax in the shroud of his blanket. "You all right?"

"All right, I guess."

Starbuck continued to study the man for a few more moments, then shook his head. "No place for you on a deal like this. How'd you happen to volunteer, anyway? Sure can't be your line of work."

"Hardly. I was a bookkeeper—back in a town near St. Louis before I came west."

"Good, comfortable way of making a living that sure beats this. Why'd you change? Looking for something better?"

"No—oblivion."

Starbuck frowned. "What?"

Walt Moody turned upon his back, drew his blanket tighter around his slight frame. "I wanted to lose myself, if I could."

"I see. . . . Trouble of some kind, I take it."

"The worst, far as I'm concerned." Moody's voice faltered, fell silent.

Shawn lay back, watched the sky light up, silhouetting the tips of the swaying pines, listened to the subsequent deep-throated grumble. Brandon no longer stood at the edge of the clearing, but was now finding himself a place to sleep beneath an overhang of brush. Rome was already curled in his wool cover an arm's reach beyond Dave Gilder. Shawn yawned, felt an easiness steal over him, wondered idly what Moody had meant, but he wouldn't press the man for an

47

explanation. If he wished to go further into it, it would be his choice.

"You think it's possible for a man to ever get away from himself?"

Starbuck stared up into the black sky and considered Walt Moody's question. "Be hard to do. A man can't get away from his own thoughts—and I expect it amounts to the same thing. That what you're trying to do?"

"Guess it is."

"Well, I doubt if you'll ever be able to do it just waiting around, looking for it. That just lets whatever it is eating at your mind have its way. You need to fill it with something else—crowd out all the old things."

"But if I can't do that—"

"Can't—or don't want to? Which is it? Maybe that's what you'd better figure out first."

Walt Moody made no reply. Shawn heard him moving about restlessly as if seeking greater comfort. He yawned again. His own eyes were getting heavy.

"I expect you're right. I'm not sure what the answer is, or that I can even find it. It's easy for a man to lie to himself."

Shawn brushed at his mouth. . . . First Able Rome, now Walt Moody . . . . . . "Just as easy to be truthful since nobody but himself knows what's in his head."

"But if a man's done something, been responsible for some terrible thing, how can he get it out of his mind?"

"I can't give you any answer to that, but I'm pretty sure the same problem's been faced by others and licked. I expect the big thing is that you've got to want to lick it, not let the guilt make a slave of you. That's always the easy way out. Self-pity is plenty cheap. It's the other way that's tough going."

48

The night came alive again with the awesome flare of electricity, shuddered with the tumbling of sound. Shawn closed his eyes.

"It's that—the guilt, that rides me so hard—"

Moody's voice seemed far away, a mere echo in a vast emptiness.

"I'd like to tell you about it—just what happened—"

The words slipped away from Starbuck, faded into silence without registering on his mind. . . . Later, he'd listen . . . later. . . .

CHAPTER 8

THE STORM HELD OFF THROUGHOUT THE NIGHT, AND then as Brandon's posse moved onto the trail that next morning under a sullen, gray sky, the first spatter of raindrops struck.

They came in a gusty blast, cold and stinging in their intensity. Immediately Starbuck halted the sorrel and drew on his slicker. A few paces away Able Rome also donned his rain gear as well as pulling on a pair of worn, leather chaps as further protection from the wet. Brandon, cursing steadily at the inconvenience, followed their example, but Moody and Gilder, not similarly equipped, were forced to choose between using their blankets or nothing. Both elected to drape themselves with the woolen covers.

Lightning, with its accompanying hammer of thunder, quiet during the early hours of the morning, again began to flood the slopes and canyons with its brilliance and rock the land with resounding echoes. There was a difference, however; where before there had been broad flashes succeeded after a pause by deep rumblings, there

49

now were swift, jagged flashes, and the thunder, crackling and deafening, came almost in the same breath.

The trail, in only short minutes, became a narrow, muddy stream bed surging with water racing downslope, washing topsoil, small rocks, loose brush and other litter before it. The horses, moving slow at best up the fairly steep grade, dropped to a yet more deliberate pace, their hides glistening in the wet, eyes showing white with each garish flare of light.

"That's the hell of this goddam country!" Brandon shouted above the howl of the storm when they paused under the partly protective bulk of a pine that overshadowed their course. "Always too much of something. It's too hot or too cold, or maybe too dry and then we're getting flooded out by a damned cloudburst that takes half the land with it."

A vivid streak of lightning slashed through the murk. A hundred yards back up the slope a tree split with a thunderous crash, and became a flaming torch. The horses began to mince nervously, frightened by the fire, the sizzling sound of water dashing against it.

Again a jagged, blue line of light split the wet gloom. A ball of fire struck high on a ridge of rocks above them, rolled a short distance and exploded against the face of a glistening butte.

Starbuck, wiping the water from his eyes, glanced at the men huddled beside him under the pine. They were all staring at the hogback as if transfixed. Thunder crackled, seemingly right upon them. He reached out, touched Harry Brandon's arm.

"We stay here or go on?"

The lawman shook his head. "Won't get no wetter riding than standing."

Shawn mentally agreed. There was the possibility

they were in the center of the downpour. Climbing higher could put them on its fringe, or perhaps entirely out of it.

A new sound began to fill the air, rising above the chatter of the drops. It was the deep, rushing roar of wild water, pent up by natural dams in the higher canyons, suddenly released and now pouring down the steep slopes for the flat land far below. Gouging and slashing, the torrents were following none of the prescribed channels cut by previous, more gentle storms, but were knifing new troughs in a turbulent, irresistible race to low ground.

The posse moved out from beneath the tree, horses reluctant, taking each step with hesitant care, fearful of the unstable footing and frightened by the persistent pushing of the swirling water around their hooves.

Shawn tried to look ahead, to determine if there were canyons coming in at right angles to the trail. If so they could expect to encounter a rushing wall of silt- and brush-laden floodwater, perhaps even come to a point where a gash had been cut in their path.

He could tell nothing about it. Rain was a gray sheet before his eyes and even when the almost continuous lightning spread its eerie, blue glow over the mountainside, his vision was limited to a dozen yards.

There was a good chance they would be spared the problem. The trail appeared to be following along a spine that lifted its way steadily toward a crest lying somewhere in the soaked distance. Very likely the canyons drained to either side of the ridge, and if so, they were in luck.

Another flaming torch appeared on the slope below them as they drew to a halt once more, this time under a shoulder of granite that extended over the trail. There was no room there for the horses, but the men, by crowding close, were able to get out of the driving drops, wipe their faces and breathe deeper.

He glanced at Dave Gilder. The man was shivering from the cold. His eyes were partly closed and water dripped steadily off the tip of his nose. Moody appeared more withdrawn than ever and there was resentment in the look he gave Shawn when his gaze met the tall rider's. Able Rome alone appeared unperturbed, his black skin shining with wet as he stared off beyond the rocks.

"Best we start leading the horses," Brandon said. "Trail gets narrower on up a ways."

Shawn agreed silently. The last quarter-mile had been dangerous. Dave Gilder, the glow of the burning tree upon him, shook his head.

"I'm figuring it'd be better to hold off, Marshal, wait for the storm to pass. This here's a pretty good place."

Dave was shouting to make himself heard above the drumming sound that filled the air. Brandon's wide shoulders shifted.

"It ain't passing—not for two, maybe three hours. And we can't wait. Them killers'll keep right on moving."

"There any caves, places like that where they could hole up?" Shawn asked.

Again the lawman stirred. "Nope, aint none they can reach for a couple of days. Trail just runs straight on to the top of the mountains with nothing on either side but slopes, same as it's been since we left camp."

At least there was no need to worry about arroyos cutting the path out from under them, Starbuck thought, but now something else was becoming apparent. Both Moody and Gilder were showing signs of strain. The constant spurts of lightning striking nearby, the crackle of thunder and the sound of rushing water coupled to the never slackening drive of the rain, were unnerving them.

He glanced at Rome, caught the man looking at him. Able forced a smile, one designed to reassert his self-assurance as opposed to the apprehension being displayed by the two others. But the smile was only on the surface and there were tight lines around his eyes.

Their anxiety was warranted and Shawn could not blame them for their concern. Being trapped in the heart of a wild storm high on a mountain while lightning crackled and shattered mighty trees as though they were matchsticks and set the earth to trembling underfoot with thunderous accompaniment, was far from a tranquil experience.

For himself he tried not to dwell on possibilities too much. He avoided such circumstances whenever possible, feeling that any man was a fool to tempt fate by exposing himself, but once involved in a situation of danger, he accepted it, realizing that there was little he could do to avoid whatever was inevitable, and the less thought he gave it, the better. Long ago he had learned that all the worrying and stewing he did affected the end result not at all.

"Let's move out—"

At Harry Brandon's order, he looked up. The marshal stepped from beneath the slanting canopy of granite, and taking up the reins of his horse, nodded.

"Could be letting up a mite at that," the lawman said. "Don't seem to be stinging so hard."

Starbuck could note little difference. The raindrops were still coming down with slashing force, the lightning continued to rip the wet pall clothing the mountain, and thunder rolled and thudded ominously. It would be good if they could find shelter, wait for a time as Dave Gilder had suggested, but he could see Brandon's point, too.

The outlaws knew that a posse was at their heels hoping to close in; they would not risk a halt, but press on regardless of conditions. With the store of gold they had killed to obtain as well as their own lives at stake, they would throw caution aside in their hurry to escape.

Starbuck peered from under the cupped shelter of his hand. The footing was slippery as mud steadily deepened on the trail, narrower here as Harry Brandon had said it would be. The lawman was well ahead of Gilder, second in line, and moving slowly. Moody followed next, with Able Rome, from choice, again bringing up the rear.

A blinding flash of lightning, striking close by, filled the air with a pungent, scorched odor. The ground rocked with the concussion of thunder.

Starbuck, hanging tight to the sorrel's reins, saw Brandon's horse balk, go to his hind legs, paw at the hammering rain with his front hooves, as if doing battle with an invisible stallion.

In the next fragment of time Walt Moody's buckskin jerked back, attempted to wheel on the narrow, slippery surface of the trail. His hindquarters slapped hard against Moody, knocked him aside. For an instant the man tottered on the edge of the ridge, mouth blared in a soundless cry of fear, and then he was gone.

CHAPTER 9

SHAWN, CLINGING TO THE SORREL'S LEATHERS WITH one hand, wheeled to the rope hanging from his saddle and jerked it free with the other. Shaking out its coils,

54

he started for the crumbling brink of the slope. Farther up the trail he could hear Gilder shouting at Brandon, informing him of the accident while he sought to control his horse and catch up the dragging reins of the buckskin.

Reaching the point where he had last seen Moody, Shawn threw his glance down the rock-studded incline. It was shining wet in the semidarkness, and a hundred feet below he could see the boiling water of a rushing arroyo where it emptied.

There was no sign of Moody. The thought crossed his mind that the man had plunged into the swollen torrent and had been swept away. And then through the rain dimmed murk his eyes picked up vague motion about halfway down. Relief coursed through him. Moody's fall had been broken by a jutting shaft of rock.

"See him?"

It was Able Rome. Starbuck nodded, and pointing in the direction of the rock, waited out a long moment for a flash of lightning. It came suddenly, filling the canyon with dazzling brilliance.

"There—just above that hump."

"I saw him," Rome said, and began to lay out his own rope. Picking up the end of Shawn's lariat, he joined them together. "It'll take them both to reach him."

Harry Brandon crowded in beside Starbuck and peered through the driving rain into the canyon. "He gone?"

"Caught on a rock."

The lawman shook his head. "Tough break, cashing in like—"

"He's not dead—I'm pretty sure I saw him move," Shawn said, eyes on Rome now looping the rope around his chest and securing it with a hard knot.

"Body was just slipping, I expect. A fall like that'd kill a man for certain." He paused, his gaze on Able. "What the hell you doing?"

"Going after him."

Brandon straightened up. "Forget it—he's dead."

"I'm not sure of that," Starbuck said.

"Well, I am . . . . No big loss anyway. Way he's been acting, I'd say he was looking for something like this and found it—besides, we ain't got the time to waste fooling around here."

"We're taking time," Shawn said quietly and rising, looked about for something solid to which he could anchor the rope. He located a juniper on the opposite side of the trail. Gnarled and storm-tested, it had withstood the elements for years, and undoubtedly would serve the purpose well.

He crossed to it at once, threw a hitch about its rough trunk, knotted it close, turned to where Rome and Brandon waited.

The lawman, his features set, faced Shawn angrily as he hurried up. "I'm giving you orders, Starbuck, we ain't taking time now. We can stop on our way back for the body—"

Shawn nodded to Rome. "All set. . . I'll ease you down slow."

"You hear me?" Brandon shouted through the pouring rain. "'He's dead—and it won't hurt to leave him."

"Alive or dead, we're bringing him up," Starbuck shot back, and bracing himself, started Able Rome's descent of the slippery grade.

The footing was treacherous. Water had soaked into the soil, converting it to a slick paste that provided no purchase for Rome's boots. Rivulets of water were

56

coursing downward in almost a solid sheet. Several times the man went down, slamming hard against the canyon's side. With the aid of the lightning, Starbuck maintained a close watch on him. He could himself become injured, in which event someone else would have to follow. He'd be the one to do it, Shawn decided. Dave Gilder would have to stay above and see to their getting back; he felt he couldn't trust Harry Brandon.

Brushing at the water clouding his eyes, he stared into the grayness of the canyon. The storm raged on, periodically filling the deep gap with blinding light and ear-splitting thunder while the rain continued to hammer at them relentlessly. The wet rope became slick between his gloved hands and he began to fight to keep his footing on the mushy soil of the trail. He turned to Gilder, hoping the man could come to his aid, but Dave was having his troubles with the nervous horses. Suddenly angered, he swung his eyes to Brandon.

"Give me some help here!" he snarled. "We're not moving on till we get him up!"

The marshal, jaw clamped shut, hesitated briefly, and then as if realizing the truth of Shawn's statement, stepped in behind him, and taking a grip on the lariat, threw his weight against the pull of Able Rome's body.

The strain on Shawn eased considerably with that and he turned his attention to the slope. In the next flash of lightning he saw Able reach the finger of rock against which Walt Moody had lodged and felt the drag on the rope slacken.

"He's reached him," he shouted over his shoulder, and going to hands and knees, stared down into the murky depths of the canyon, searching for a sign from Rome as to Moody's condition.

It was difficult to determine what was taking place.

The rain was like a curtain and he could make out only blurred motion on Able's part. Then, faint through the howling storm, he heard a yell. There was a tug on the rope. Rome was signaling.

Shawn got to his feet hurriedly, braced himself. "Haul in!" he shouted to Brandon.

Together they began to draw in the rope. It would have been a simple task for one of the horses, but the narrowness of the trail and its condition plus the nervousness of the animals made that out of the question. But it was not too difficult.

Shortly the head and shoulders of the man appeared at the lip of the canyon. Starbuck dug his heels deep into the mud, set himself and barked at the lawman.

"Get him!"

Brandon stepped around Shawn, bent over the limp form of Moody and dragged him up onto the trail. Immediately Starbuck moved to him, began to remove the rope looped under his armpits. Moody stared up at him from his tired eyes.

"Ain't dead," Brandon muttered, hunching over him. "Banged up plenty, but he's alive."

Shawn returned to the edge of the slope. Locating Rome, he bunched the soaked rope and tossed it at the near-invisible shape crouched beside the shaft of rock. After a moment he felt a jerk on the line, Starbuck again braced himself, called to Brandon.

"Let's haul him up."

Rising from where he knelt beside Walt Moody, the lawman took his position behind Starbuck and once more they began to retrieve the rain-slicked line. It was easier. Where Moody had been unable to give any assistance and offered only dead weight, Able Rome helped by digging his feet into the slope and grabbing

58

onto the rocks and few brush clumps that were available.

In a short time he was on the trail, plastered with mud that was slowly washing away under the driving raindrops. He grinned at Shawn as he began to loosen the coil about his body and in his eyes there was a look of satisfaction, as if he had demonstrated an ability others might not have suspected.

Shawn smiled back and turned to Moody. The dazed, worn stare was gone from his eyes and he had pulled himself to a sitting position. Pain distorted his features as he felt at his left arm.

"You hurt bad?" Starbuck asked, crouching beside him.

Dave Gilder was yelling again, this time wanting to know about Moody's condition. Rome, coiling the ropes, moved toward him to give a report.

"Only—my arm," Moody replied.

"Lucky," Harry Brandon said gruffly. "Mighty goddam lucky, I'd say. Was the mud being soft that did it."

Walt started to rise, winced at the effort. Shawn, taking him by his uninjured arm, assisted him to his feet.

"Got to be getting on," the marshal continued, mopping at his streaming face. "You make it?"

Lips tight, Moody nodded and turned to start up the trail. Starbuck halted him.

"That arm's got to be set."

Again Walt moved his head. "I know that—but later on, when we stop."

"He's right," Brandon said. "Hard to do it here on this ridge. Farther up there'll be a place where we can pull off."

"How far?"

"Couple hours—maybe less."

Shawn peered closely at Moody through the grey curtain. "Can you stand it that long?"

"Guess so—"

Then let's get started," Brandon said briskly, crossing to his horse. "We lost too damned much time already. Going to have to hurry things some."

Moody stared at the marshal woodenly and then faced Starbuck. "Walking's going to be a little hard—mind looking after my animal?"

"I'll see to him," Shawn answered. "'Just hang tight until we can get to where that arm can got fixed."

Walt Moody smiled wearily. "Fixing it will be easy. It's what's inside me that I can't do anything about."

Starbuck watched him head on up the trail and then crossed to where Dave Gilder waited with the horses. The injured man's words trickled slowly through his mind. Whatever the trouble was that plagued Moody, it weighed heavily on him.

He recalled that Moody had been about to tell him. take him into his confidence the night before, but he dropped off to sleep. Likely that had turned the man inward more than ever. He'd try and square it, explain that exhaustion had simply gotten the best of him, and that he'd like to hear about his problem—and perhaps be of help. Maybe Walt would listen to an apology and open up. That was what he needed to do—talk, unload, get whatever it was eating at him out into the open.

The rain had finally ceased, leaving behind a damp, chilled world of dripping trees and soggy ground. Walt Moody sat on a rotting log in a small clearing off the trail where they had halted for the night, and watched the other men moving about making camp. Starbuck and Rome had taken their slickers, hooked them together and suspended them, lean-to fashion, between four trees for a shelter under which they could spend the hours until morning.

Gilder, his eyes sunk deep in his head as the craving that everybody by now recognized, gripped him, was endeavoring to scare up dry wood for a fire and was not having much success. The marshal, irritated by the delay that the storm and the accident had occasioned, was a short distance up the trail, looking to the south as if hopeful of catching sight of the outlaws.

Walt Moody shifted, carefully holding his repaired arm with the right hand so that it would not move. Starbuck and the black man had done a good job setting it and pinning it firmly between the straight sticks they used as splints. It throbbed dully, like a bad toothache, but he guessed he'd live through it.

For what?

The question seeped its bitter way into his brain. Why the hell couldn't he have done the job up right and tumbled all the way down that damned slope into the floodwater—and ended it all once and for good? No—it was his luck to have a rock waiting there to catch him, keep him alive. . . . Nothing ever went his way.

Morose, he watched Starbuck and Able Rome now busy stretching a rope near where the fire was to be built so that the soaked blankets could be dried. The pair worked together smoothly and efficiently, talking little, each seemingly aware of the other's capabilities.

He had thanked Starbuck for his part in dragging him out of that canyon—had to remember to thank the colored man also. He'd been the one who did the climbing down with the rope. . . . He'd say what he should when they all gathered around the fire if Gilder ever got one going.

But the thanks would be for nothing as far as he was concerned. He'd a thousand times prefer to be dead and floating down that arroyo than sitting where he was, alive, able to think and a prisoner of all the tormenting recollections that were stuck fast to his mind, like bottom land chiggers, and never let him rest.

Yesterday—last night to be exact—when he and Starbuck had been talking, he had sensed a sympathetic and perhaps understanding heart on the part of the tall, hard-jawed rider, and something had come over him, a lift—a hope; and for the first time since it had all happened it seemed he could see a light at the end of the interminable tunnel of despair through which he had been groping for so long. . . . But it had turned out just as things always did for him.

He had told Starbuck of Rozella, of what they had meant to each other, and how she had died that terrible day when they had been boating on the lake. It had been his fault, cutting up, acting the fool the way he did, and then when the small craft overturned, he had clung to it, paralyzed, horrified and unnerved by her screams, powerless to save her.

He was no swimmer but he could have saved her. He could have gotten to her, managed somehow to drag her back to the boat where they both could have hung on until help arrived—but he hadn't. Instead he'd just stayed there, fingers locked to the bottom of the craft, listening to her piteous cries and watching while the dark water swallowed her. He knew then that he was a coward.

And later, when the full realization of the tragedy hit him, he knew also that Rozella was dead by his own hand as surely as if he'd held a pistol to her temple and pulled the trigger.

At that point in the narration he had paused. It came to him that he was baring his soul to the wind; Starbuck had fallen asleep, had heard none of what had been said.

That had finished it for him. He had never before unburdened himself to another in his desperate search for understanding—now he would never do so again.

But it was done and he was back, mentally, where he started, still facing the accusing fingers that pointed at him from a hundred dark hiding places in his mind, still torn by doubt and the fear of fear that constantly reproved him.

No one was ever interested in another's troubles, anyway; he should have remembered that. . . . He'd find his own answers alone—unaided.

CHAPTER 10

THEY HELD THE FIRE TO A SMALL SIZE, NOT JUST because dry wood was scarce and available only by seeking out the larger rocks and probing about beneath them, but also to avoid a repeat performance on the part of the outlaws; this time a rifle bullet could find a human target.

The evening meal over and the blankets hanging on the leeward side of the flames where a combination of smoke and heat was slowly accomplishing their drying, Starbuck seated himself within the limited fan of light and glanced to the sky. The overcast had broken to some extent and a few stars were visible, but the threat of more rain was still there.

He sighed heavily, hoped it would not come to pass;

much more water pouring down upon the mountain would make the trail impassable and all their efforts to overtake the outlaws would go for nothing. Too, Walt Moody should be taken to a doctor as soon as possible; the medical attention he and Able Rome had provided was crude and only of an emergency nature at best.

He glanced at Walt Moody. He was hunched against a pine, head slung forward, arms cradled, apparently sleeping. He'd had a bad time of it, going over the cliff, walking for all that time with the injured arm uncared for and then withstanding the treatment necessary to accord it without uttering more than an occasional groan. He should be sent back to Wolf Crossing; he would be of little use to the posse, anyway. He'd talk to Brandon about it in the morning, Shawn decided.

Able Rome, his features reflecting the weariness that rode him, came up from where the horses had been picketed. Nodding to Shawn and Gilder , and glancing at the dozing Moody, he sat down, leaned forward to capture some of the fire's warmth.

"Where is he—the marshal?" he asked after a time.

Gilder, scrubbing agitatedly at the stubble of whiskers on his chin, said, "Up the trail. Trying to spot them killers, I reckon."

Rome grunted. "Surprised he didn't want to keep moving."

Only the exhausted condition of the horses had prevented the lawman from insisting on it, Starbuck guessed. Between the storm and Moody's accident they had made little progress that day. Probably the realization that the outlaws could have done no better was the major factor in persuading him to lay over for the night.

Gilder turned his strained features to Shawn. "You

figure there's a chance we can catch up to them tomorrow and head back to town?"

"Could be. Don't think they're too far ahead."

"God—I'm hoping so." Dave Gilder muttered in an exhausted tone.

Rome picked up one of the empty cups setting nearby, filled it half full from the simmering pot of coffee and offered it to the trembling man.

"Ease off," he said quietly.

Gilder took the cup, held it to his lips and gulped its contents, shivering uncontrollably.

"Thanks," he murmured, and hunching forward, buried his face in cupped hands.

"Everybody's got a problem," Able observed quietly, shifting his eyes to Starbuck. "Comes with living, it seems."

Shawn shrugged, and glanced up as Harry Brandon came down the short slope from the trail and stepped into the ring of firelight.

"Any sign?"

The lawman shook his head. "Naw—nothing, but they ain't far. Can't be, not with all this rain and the trail being in the shape it is." He reached into his pocket, drew out the almost empty bottle of whiskey and took a long pull of it. "We'll nail 'em in the morning."

David Gilder stirred restlessly. A small sound escaped his throat. Shawn spoke up quickly.

"Be glad to go after them now—the two of us, if you figure it's the thing to do."

"No sense in it. Like I said before, they can't do nothing but stick to this trail. Tomorrow'll be soon enough." The lawman moved in closer to the fire. Bottle in hand, he hunched. "Be a fool risk, anyways, trying to get to them in the dark."

Starbuck watched Brandon take another swallow of liquor. He disagreed as to the merits of closing in on the outlaws under cover of night, but it was Brandon's posse and the lawman had made it clear he was running it.

"There's something I want to say," the marshal continued, wiping his mouth with the back of a hand. "We see them, I want every man jack of you to open up—shoot. Don't hold off."

Shawn drew himself up slowly. "You're not giving them a chance to throw down their guns?"

"Hell, no! Be a waste of breath. I know them birds—they won't give up—and they'll kill you if you don't kill them first."

"How about Starbuck's brother?" Rome asked. "Ain't he one of them?"

"Who knows—and I sure'n hell ain't waltzing up to them and asking!"

"Then I will," Shawn said, "or are you going to say now that it was all a lie to start with?"

Brandon wagged his head. "No, I wasn't lying to you. One of them is Ben Snow—just like I told you."

"Then I'm going to do some talking before there's any shooting—"

"The hell you will!" Brandon shouted, his face hardening. "You'll do what I tell you—all of you will! Now maybe one of them is your brother and maybe he ain't, it don't make no difference. They're all killers and I ain't taking no chances. I'm telling you again—and by God I'm heading up this posse—when we jump them, start shooting and shooting to kill. I make myself plain?"

Starbuck remained silent. There was still a strong doubt in his mind that Ben would be found with the

66

outlaws, but the slim possibility that he could would not permit him to obey the lawman's orders. . . . He'd simply wait, somehow find a way to make sure before it was too late.

"How's the cripple doing?" Brandon asked then, jerking his thumb at Moody.

"Needs a doctor. Best you send him back to town in the morning."

"He can wait," the lawman said bluntly. "He's got one good arm he can use. Besides, I expect we'll all be heading back before the day's over."

"You're mighty sure of them," Able Rome said, studying the marshal closely.

Brandon tipped the bottle to his lips, swallowed, smiled. "Sure enough," he replied, and lowering the container, gauged its contents. Little more than one drink remained. Still grinning, he turned to Dave Gilder.

"And how're you doing, mister?"

Gilder stirred helplessly. "Not—so good."

"That so? Well, maybe you could use this here last swallow," Brandon said, and leaning forward, waved the bottle in front of the man's nose.

Gilder jerked back, face contorted, eyes bright. "No—well, I can't—"

"Slop it down! Sure won't hurt none."

"Trying not—been fighting it—"

"Ain't nothing better for a man on a cold, wet night."

Dave squirmed, turned his head. His mouth was working convulsively and there was a wildness to him.

All yours—if you want it," Brandon said in a taunting voice. "And there ain't no more this side of the Crossing!"

Starbuck, unable to endure the torture Brandon was putting Gilder through any further, came to his feet. His

67

hand swept down, struck the bottle, knocked it from the lawman's grasp, sent it shattering on the rocks.

Eyes flaring with anger, Brandon sprang upright. "What the hell you think you're doing?" he demanded.

Shawn's cold gaze locked with the lawman's. "You want to play games, try *me*."

Brandon's hulking figure hung motionless against the darkness for a long moment, and then his thick shoulders came down. He forced a smile, brushed at his mustache, nodded.

"Just having a little fun with the sot. . . . Not meaning no harm."

"That kind of fun we can do without," Starbuck replied, and turned to the blankets, stirring in the fresh breeze.

The woolen covers had dried. Pulling them off the ropes, he tossed one to Rome, another to Dave Gilder, and then crossing to Moody, laid the third on the sleeping man's knees. Walt roused, stared about numbly, and then taking the blanket, drew it about himself.

Shawn retraced his steps to the line, collected the remaining covers, and draping one over his shoulder, handed the other to the lawman.

"We heading out early?" he asked, settling down.

"Sunrise," the marshal said and crossed to the opposite side of the fire where he could be to himself.

Dave Gilder hugged his blanket tighter to his body and shivered, but it was not from the night's cold; rather, it came from an inner chill. He shifted his feverish eyes to the bits of broken glass scattered around the stones he had arranged for the fire. The strong smell of whiskey still hung in the air, tantalizing, taunting him cruelly.

68

God, how he had wanted that drink—and Brandon had known the depth of his need!

But Starbuck—damn him, too—had snatched it away from him just as he was about to give in, surrender to the raving, unholy thirst that was ravaging him from scalp to toe.

He'd wanted it in the worst way—and he hadn't wanted it, knowing that once that first drop had slid down his throat he would be off once more—lost again. But wasn't it better to be lost and alive—than dead?

He groaned, again clutched at the blanket as he glanced about at the sleeping men around him. They didn't know what it was like, this whiskey fever that possessed him. They maybe thought they did, but no man could really know unless he'd been through it himself. And that goddam Brandon, that stinking, lousy excuse for a lawman, teasing him the way he had! The smell of the whiskey when he'd held it under his nose had almost turned him inside out. He wished now he'd made a grab for it, gulped it down before Brandon could snatch it away—if that's what he intended to do—and likely it was.

What the hell was the use of fighting it? He'd never lick it, never win. No matter how hard and often he'd tried, he always found himself waking up one day with all the demons in hell running loose inside his head, gut-sick and more dead than alive.

The real answer, he guessed, lay not in waking up someday, just passing out in the back of some saloon and never coming out of it. . . . But that meant never seeing Felicity and the boys again and he'd not been able to get that hope out of his mind.

He supposed that was the one reason for the continual warfare that half of him waged with the other half—that

69

solitary, shining hope that someday it would all be as it had once been; but was keeping alive that hope worth the price he was paying? Right now he doubted it and that disturbed him, for never before had any such uncertainty filtered into his mind.

Was he slipping farther down, going deeper into the black morass of alcoholic nothingness? Was he losing sight of the only things that meant something to him?

Exhausted beyond the point of needing sleep, Dave Gilder stirred, shakily reached for the cup Able Rome had handed him earlier. Maybe another swallow or two of Starbuck's black, bitter coffee would stifle the torment within him.

A tremor shook him. A small portion of the broken bottle lay near the blackened pot in its curve a teaspoon or so of golden liquid winked up at him.

He let the cup fall, extended a forefinger toward the bit of glass. . . . Just a taste, that's all he wanted—all he needed. It would quiet his nerves, let him settle down. Yes, just a taste. . . . It wouldn't hurt. . . .

An anguished sound burst from his lips. His hand swept down, fingers scooping through the ashes and bits of charred twigs, sent it showering over the curve of glass and its tempting contents. And then folding his arms across his knees, Dave Gilder lowered his head and wept like a child.

CHAPTER 11

THE PREDAWN HOUR WAS COLD, AND BECAUSE OF THE shortage of dry wood, the fire was large enough only to boil coffee and fry bacon and grease bread. The meal was eaten and camp broken in the deep silence of men

70

chilled to the bone and in ill humor.

But later the sun caught them moving up the trail in single file, and as its warmth spread subtly over the mountain and seeped into their bodies, they began to loosen up and some of the hostility faded from their manner.

Starbuck, intentionally choosing the second-in-line position behind Harry Brandon where he would be able to see the outlaws at the same moment the lawman located them, scoured his mind for some plan by which he could get to the three before the marshal could carry out his threat to shoot first and ask no questions.

He felt sure Ben would not be one of the killers; Brandon had voiced the possibility only as a means to enlist him in the posse, but he was not so convinced that he would blindly accept the conviction without making an effort to be certain. Ben *could* have changed—and he must know for certain, one way or the other, before any shooting was done.

Just how he could do so was the question. He might break away from the posse, circle ahead and put himself well out in front and thereby be able to spot the outlaws first. But that would be difficult The trail still clung to the crest of a narrow hogback and the slopes dropping away on either side were both steep and exceedingly slippery from the rain. Footing for either man or horse was impossible.

Also, to determine definitely if one of the men was Ben, he would have to move in close to them. Even then it would be only a guess. Ben likely had changed much in ten years, and from a distance there would be only a hoped-for family resemblance to go by. To be absolutely certain, it would be necessary to draw near enough to talk and look for the small scar that could be

71

found above his brother's left eye.

Starbuck shrugged in impatience. There seemed no way other than persuading Brandon to close in quietly on the men and capture them rather than to shoot them down when sighted.

Spurring the sorrel nearer to the lawman, he said, "Marshal, I'd like to make you a deal."

Brandon, the incident of the whiskey bottle plainly a galling recollection still in his mind, half turned on his saddle.

"On what?" he asked sourly.

"The outlaws. When we spot them, how about letting me go ahead, slip in close and see if I can recognize my brother. You keep them covered and I'll offer to let them throw down their guns while I'm having my look—"

"Forget it, Starbuck," the lawman snapped, his mouth a hard line. "You'd never be able to get that close."

"It would be me taking the chance."

"Buying yourself a grave'd be more like it."

"It's my neck."

"And getting them's my responsibility. Like as not your messing around would fix it so's they could make a run for it—get away."

"Not if you had them covered," Shawn persisted, stubbornly. Brandon was silent for a brief time, then he shook his head. "No, I ain't risking losing them."

Anger welled through Starbuck. "You do some thinking about it, Marshal." he said in a level voice.

The lawman came fully around, gave Shawn's taut features a calculating appraisal. Reading the determination in the tall rider's eyes, he nodded slowly.

"All right, I'll think on it," he said curtly, and squared himself on his saddle.

Starbuck dropped back into his place in the slow-moving cavalcade, glancing at the others as he did. Dave Gilder, drawn and desolate, looking as if he'd had no sleep at all, was behind him. Moody, slumped to one side, nursing his arm, came next. Able Rome, as before, brought up the rear. His solemn eyes met Shawn's, held, expressing nothing.

The thought came into Starbuck's mind as he rocked gently with the motion of the sorrel and listened to the quiet *thunk* of his hooves on the mushy ground, that turning on Brandon, taking charge of the posse himself might be the solution. The marshal was handling the matter unlike any lawman he had ever known—planning to murder the men he pursued without giving them a chance to surrender—and that actually was ample reason to assume command.

It wouldn't matter to the townspeople who had expressed their dislike for their marshal, or to the Paradise mine, which was interested only in recovering its stolen gold. All that mattered to either faction was the apprehension of the outlaws.

But he would need the support of the rest of the posse and that was something he could not be sure of. Moody was more or less out of it, although he could use a gun, if need be; the two others, unstable, and unpredictable, were hard to measure.

Gilder, in his present state of mind, could fall apart completely or he might, in consideration of what he believed to be his best interests, stand by Brandon. That could also apply to Able Rome—a man bent on carving a niche for himself in an unfriendly world, regardless of opposition—or tradition.

But most important of all he would be breaking the law himself by deposing the marshal, and that he did not relish the thought of doing. No matter how he looked at it, Harry Brandon was a duly elected representative of the law, the merits of his judgment, good or bad, notwithstanding. To oppose him meant defiance of the law and that was something that ran counter to Shawn Starbuck's nature and beliefs. . . . Best he give the idea serious deliberation before making such a move.

Reaching up, he released the top button of his brush jacket. The day was warming rapidly and signs of the heavy rain were beginning to disappear. Pools of water, yet lay on the trail and brush and trees on the slopes still glistened wetly in the bright sunlight, but such evidence would all have disappeared by sundown.

Overheard in the cloudless sky an eagle soared effortlessly on broad wings, and here and there on the upper slopes irregular patches of gold marked the location of aspen groves. They were in high country, Shawn realized, and still climbing. It would seem they should be topping out the range and dropping off onto its yonder side before too long. It was difficult to tell, however, just where that point would be because the timber growth was dense and visibility limited to a short distance.

Near noon they reached a small clearing that lay off the trail to the left. More rock was in evidence now and the timber had thinned to some extent, indicating they were drawing near the summit.

"Get some coffee made," Brandon directed, swinging down onto the flat and dismounting. His mien had changed to one of cheerfulness and he seemed to have forgotten the cross-purpose words he'd had with Starbuck. "Hard climb coming up. Horses need a bit of rest."

Shawn and the others had followed suit, grunting a little as they came off their saddles. It had been a slow, tedious climb and leaving the leather was a welcome break.

Taking up the sack of grub and cooking gear, Starbuck motioned Walt Moody to a log where he could sit and be out of the way, and then moved to the center of the clearing. Brandon, rifle in hand, doubled back to the trail for his customary look at the country ahead. Rome led the horses off to one side and Dave Gilder began his quest for dry wood.

It was more plentiful among the rocks, and shortly he had a brisk fire going for Shawn to set his containers of water over. A piñon jay appeared and began to flit nervously about in the nearby trees. His noisy scolding quickly attracted others and soon a dozen or more of the slate blue birds were voicing their harsh disapproval of intruders, from the safety of the pines and spruces.

Shawn, hunched over the flames, frying bacon and chunks of potatoes he'd baked that previous night while they lazed around the campfire, glanced up as Rome paused before him.

"I heard you arguing with the marshal about your brother. He willing to let you go first?"

"Hasn't said so."

"Still aims to shoot first—then look?"

Starbuck nodded. "I don't much think my brother's with them, but I'd like to be sure."

Rome drew out his cigarette sack. "That's not the way the law's supposed to work, anyway. We ought to give them a chance to quit."

"That's the way I see it, too, but I figured, having a personal interest, I could be looking at it one-sided."

Starbuck hesitated, then said: "If I was to take over from the marshal, handle this the way I think a lawman should, where would you stand?"

75

"With you," Rome said promptly. "Right's right, and Brandon's sure wrong—planning murder the way he is."

Shawn stirred the contents of the spider slowly. "I'm not one to buck the law. I always believed it was due respect regardless of who wore the star, and that's got me trying to convince myself that what I'm thinking of doing is for the sake of the law and not because of my brother."

Rome turned to Dave Gilder, coming back into the clearing with another armload of wood. "We'd like for you to hear this. We don't figure the marshal's acting like a marshal," he said. "The way we see it, he ought to give those outlaws a chance to give in—not shoot them down."

"It amounts to murder," Moody said from his place on the log.

Shawn glanced at the man. He had assumed him to be dozing and unaware of the conversation.

Gilder dropped the firewood, rubbed at his jaw nervously. "I—I don't know. They ain't nothing but killers. Not deserving of decent treatment."

"The law says every man's entitled to a fair trial," Rome pointed out. "Or don't you figure the law ought to apply to every man?"

Gilder stared at Able bleakly. "Sure I do, only when—"

The sudden smash of rifle shots echoed through the canyons and across the plateaus. Starbuck, features grim, leaped to his feet. Drawing his pistol, he ran toward the trail.

"No use talking about it," he shouted. "Brandon's, spotted them!"

CHAPTER 12

THERE HAD BEEN NO DISTANT, ANSWERING GUNSHOTS, only those coming from Harry Brandon's rifle. Anger surged through Starbuck. The lawman had gone ahead with his plan, opened up on the outlaws without giving them a chance to surrender. If one of them was Ben—

He swore harshly, rushed on toward what appeared to be a rocky summit a hundred yards farther up the trail. The others were close behind him—Able Rome to his right, Gilder to the left and Walt Moody, holding his broken arm slightly forward to prevent it from striking against his body as he ran, in the center and to the rear. Despite his injury, Walt was doing his part.

Brandon appeared suddenly on the crest, stepping from behind a wagon-size boulder that stood at the end of a straggling pile of lesser rocks. The lawman waved vigorously, signaling them to him.

"Got them boxed in a coulee—bottom of the slope!" he shouted as they drew near.

Stiff with anger, Shawn strode by him to the edge of the formation and threw his glance down the grade. A man lay in a small clearing at its base not far below. His hat had come off to reveal a shock of corn yellow hair. Both arms were outstretched, his hands empty. There was no doubt that he was dead.

"Opened up on me when I showed myself."

At Brandon's words Starbuck spun. His jaw was set to a hard line and his eyes were narrowed.

"We heard only your shots," he said, accusation in his voice.

"You calling me a liar?" the lawman demanded.

Starbuck's shoulders stirred. He should have expected

Brandon to do as he'd planned. But it was too late to do anything about it now.

"The rest of them still down there?"

Brandon, head thrust forward belligerently, said, "Hell yes, they're down there. You don't believe it, step out there into the open."

Shawn moved to the forward edge of the rocks, leveled his pistol and pressed off a shot. The bullet struck in the center of the coulee, showered twigs and dirt on the dead outlaw. Immediately two rifles laid their quick answers across the rolling echoes loosed by his weapon.

Brandon, mouth pulled into a sneer, nodded. "Reckon that ought to satisfy you."

"That they're there—not that they started the shooting," Starbuck said coldly and turned back to the rocks.

"You men in the coulee—throw down your guns and step out where we can see you!" he called.

"Go to hell!" The reply floated lazily up the slope.

"You don't have a chance. Quit now and we'll see you get a fair trial."

There was no response. Shawn brushed at the sweat on his face. "Is one of you Ben Starbuck? I'm his brother—Shawn."

The rifles cracked again. Bullets caromed off the rocks with a weird, shrilling sound.

"You done?" Brandon asked in a low, scornful voice. "You ready for me to take over, Mister Starbuck?"

Shawn pulled back from the rocks into the little hollow in which they'd gathered. The lawman had voided any possibility of talking the outlaws into surrendering. As for Ben, he was still unsure—but he had done all he could.

"It's your posse," he said.

"I'll be obliged if you'll keep remembering that," the marshal replied, his tone heavy with sarcasm. He swung to Gilder and the others. "Now, I want you to spread out, start pouring lead into that coulee. Good chance we'll wing them two that's left."

Able Rome immediately moved off to the right. Gilder and Walt Moody cut to the opposite direction. Shawn returned to where he had first looked down the slope, a place near center. He could see little point in following out the lawman's plan; it would serve only to pin down the outlaws, eventually force them to abandon their positions, fall back into the surrounding brush and make a run for it.

But Brandon could have a plan in mind that he was not making known, and stationing himself, he rested his weapon on the flat, top surface of the boulder behind which he stood and began to fire. The others also opened up, as did the cornered outlaws, and for a time the mountains were filled with the thunder of guns.

"Hold up!" Brandon yelled, finally. "We ain't doing no good—just wasting ammunition."

The lawman drew back to where the massive pile of rocks gave him full protection from the men below. Pulling off his hat, he mopped at his forehead, glanced around.

"I figure they're forted up behind something that we ain't seeing. Got to get at them from the side." He paused, pointed to a lesser scatter of rocks at the far end of narrow plateau to their right. "Want one of you to get over there. Maybe we can get them in a sort of crossfire."

Shawn frowned. There was no way a man could reach the point indicated without fully exposing himself.

"It'd be suicide," he snapped. "Nobody could cross that flat without getting cut down. Be smarter for us to separate, work our way around in a circle, come in on that coulee from all sides."

"They'd pull out on us, if we was to try that, and it'd take too much time."

"It'll beat getting somebody killed—"

"Goddammit!" Brandon exploded. "You trying to run this outfit again?"

"Start showing sense and—"

"I can make it," Rome cut in abruptly. "Cover me."

Shawn whirled to the man. Able's eyes were bright and there was the look on his round face of a small boy about to take a dare.

"Don't be a fool—you won't get halfway—"

"Move out—you're covered!" Brandon shouted, and hurrying to the rocks began to fire into the coulee.

Rome, flinging a quick smile at Starbuck, darted into the open. Bent low, he started across the rounded surface of the ridge-like flat, running erratically, dodging from side to side. The outlaws opened up at once. Bullets dug into the, ground at his feet, spanged off into space as they glanced against rocks.

Brandon's shots, supported by those of the remaining posse members, did nothing to deter them. Evidently they were well protected, as the lawman had thought.

"He's hit!"

At Moody's yell, Shawn came about. Rome was down on one knee, was struggling to crawl, gain the protection of the rocks. Another slug smashed into him, knocked him flat. He stirred feebly, tried to rise.

"I'll get him," Walt Moody said quietly and holstering his pistol, rushed out onto the flat.

"No!" Starbuck yelled. "Too late to help—"

80

But Moody, following Able Rome's example, was already beyond the rocks, running fast, swerving from side to side. Almost to Rome's unmoving shape, he hesitated in stride as a bullet caught him. His body jerked as half a dozen more drove in him, spun him around and sent him sprawling.

An abrupt hush fell across the slope. Harry Brandon cursed in a low voice. "Goddammit to hell."

Shawn stared at him. "What did you expect? They didn't stand a chance out there."

Brandon shook his head, spat. "The nigger might've made it—with a little luck."

He swung back to the rock looked down into the coulee. "Ain't but one thing to do, he murmured as if thinking aloud. "That's slip up on them from the side."

Shawn stirred wearily. It was what he had wanted to do at the beginning but the marshal had waved off the suggestion. Now, after the lives of the two men had been spent, he was willing to try it.

"Little late to think of that," he said coldly.

Brandon shrugged. "Nobody said this was going to be a picnic. They knew what they was liable to run into."

"Maybe, but I don't think they counted on dying for nothing."

Starbuck mulled his own words over in his mind. Able Rome had seemed uncommonly anxious to take the risk that had cost him his life. Had he, in those brief moments, visualized some goal he felt was worth an attempt to reach? To prove himself the equal or better than any white man had been an obsession with him; had this been the means of confirming that avowal?

And Walt Moody . . . whatever it was that had twisted and tormented him and made of him a morose, frustrated man had been washed away by his act of bravery. Shawn wished now that he had been able to talk more with him, that he had not failed him that night by falling asleep. Perhaps he could have helped—and he would have had a better understanding of the man.

"You two stay put here," Brandon said, leaning his empty rifle against the rocks. His voice was low, firm. "That's a order."

Starbuck turned his attention on the lawman. "You going down there after them?"

"I aim to circle, come in from behind. Every little bit you throw a few shots into that coulee, make them think we're still up here. Understand?"

Shawn nodded.

"I get things set, I'll yell for you—and the both of you come running down that slope fast as you can. That clear?"

"We'll be ready," Starbuck said, glancing at Gilder.

"Just don't waste no time when you hear me," the lawman said, and cutting back to the trail, turned off and disappeared into the brush and trees.

CHAPTER 13

STARBUCK MADE HIS WAY BACK INTO THE ROCKS AND looked toward the coulee. The dead outlaw still lay as he had fallen. There were no signs of the others. He turned as Dave Gilder moved in beside him.

"Think they're still down there?"

For a reply Shawn pressed off two quick shots into the clearing. Instantly the outlaws returned a barrage of bullets that whined and thudded as they struck the boulders.

Gilder grinned wryly. "Reckon that's as good a

answer as a man could want." He lay back, eyes on the bodies of Moody and Able Rome. "I wish't we could drag them off there. Ain't right, letting them lay."

"Nothing we can do about it now."

"I know that. . . Sure too bad. Like you said, died for nothing."

To our way of thinking, perhaps so, Shawn thought, but he was not so certain how Rome and Moody looked at it. But he didn't feel like going into it with Gilder.

"Sure hate that about your brother. Wasn't no reason why the marshal couldn't've let you find out for sure whether he was down there before he started shooting. You think he'd a answered you, if he was one of them that's left?"

"Hard to say," Starbuck replied. "Pretty sure he would." Well off to the west and high in the heavens, two dark shapes were wheeling lazily, drifting closer. . . Buzzards.

"Well, if he is, reckon there ain't much chance of you ever seeing him alive again. Brandon'll kill them both when he gets to them."

Starbuck nodded. Ben would have answered his call, he was sure, unless he had turned his back irrevocably on the family. He reckoned he should have gone with Harry Brandon but if he had done so Gilder would be alone in the rocks and there was no assurance that he could be depended on.

Dave, however, seemed to have changed for the better. The coming to grips with the killers, the shooting, the deaths of Rome and Moody and the hard, thrusting tension that went with it all appeared to have had a salutary effect.

His features were not so haggard, the bleak desperation had left his eyes and a stability had come over him. Shawn glanced to the sky again. There were four buzzards now and they were much nearer. He jerked his thumb at the dark, broad-winged silhouettes.

"They're moving in."

Gilder swore, raised his pistol and fired several times at the scavengers. The birds seemed not to notice.

"Just got to get them two off there," Gilder said worriedly. "You think, if I was to get a rope, we might—"

"The way they're laying there's nothing we could throw a loop over."

Dave swore. "Must be something we can do."

Starbuck loosened his collar. Heat was beginning to build in the rocks and the evidence of rain, where the sun could get to it, was vanishing. In among the trees and brush it was a different story; soft mud would still be underfoot and the foliage of the growth would be wet with the moisture that had fallen.

"We keep shooting at those buzzards we'll hold them off for awhile," he said, and then turning to the rocks, fired three more bullets into the coulee. As before, the response from the outlaws was immediate.

"How long you figure it'll take Brandon to get down there?" Gilder asked.

"Be slow going, and he'll have to circle wide, come in from the side. Thirty minutes, I'd say."

"Ought to be about there, then."

Shawn made no reply. He glanced once more at the soaring vultures. They were staying high, not following their usual pattern of gradual descent. It could mean they had spotted movement—possibly Brandon or the outlaws—and were holding off. At once he turned to the coulee, emptied his pistol into the small brush-bound area. Gilder added three more bullets and then sank

84

back to watch Starbuck reload and fill his own weapon while the outlaws hammered at the rocks with their rifles.

"I've been wanting to thank you for last night," he said after a time.

Shawn paused. "Forget it. Brandon was out of line."

"I cussed you some, too, for doing it—got to tell you that because I sure wanted that drink. Then I was glad you done it. . . . I reckon you know I've got trouble with—with—"

"Whiskey," Starbuck said flatly, bringing it out into the open where it belonged. "You're not alone. Plenty others with the same problem."

Gilder toyed with the empty brass cartridges he had removed from his pistol. "I reckon so. A man always feels like it's only him having a bad time of it, though. It's a regular sickness."

"Same with everybody else that's fighting it—and you're the only doctor who can cure it."

Dive shifted nervously, tossed the spent casings into the brush. "It's not the first time I've been told that."

"I know it's easy for me to say it, but it's the truth. You're the only man alive who can make you lay off a bottle."

Gilder swore, brushed at his lips as if the mere talking of it was arousing a thirst within him. "It ain't that I haven't tried—God knows that! Got off it a hundred times—more, but I always end up right back where I started. It cost me my wife, my boys—my home—and they meant plenty to me. You think I wouldn't leave it alone so's I could get them back, if I could?"

Starbuck considered the man quietly, knowing what he would say would be brutal and cut deep.

"Maybe, inside, you don't want them back as much as

you claim."

Dave Gilder started visibly. "The devil—" he began and then fell silent. He rubbed at his mouth again, lowered his head. "I'd give anything if I could lick it, but it's got such a hold on me I can't do nothing. Man that ain't been through it just plain don't know what a hell it is."

"Every man's got some kind of a private hell. Whiskey's not the only one."

Starbuck half turned, threw two shots into the clearing. Rifles crackled as he came back around, swung his glance to the vultures. They were circling at a high level and there was an even dozen of them now. It must be Harry Brandon moving along the edge of the slope that was keeping them back. . . . The lawman should have reached the coulee by then, it seemed.

"What you said about me not wanting to quit drinking bad enough—I think I do, but maybe that's it. Maybe I could want to more only I don't realize it. How the hell's a man know when he's tying his best?"

"Something else that only a man can answer for himself. . . . Brandon ought to be close enough by now. Time we laid a barrage into that clearing, gave him some help. Do your aiming at what you can see—the marshal could be in that brush and we don't want to hit him."

Gilder checked the cylinder of his pistol and moved up beside Shawn in the rocks. They opened fire together, thoroughly lacing the small circle of ground with lead. Their shots were returned instantly and once more the canyons and slopes rocked with continuing echoes.

"If Brandon was there, that should've fixed it so's he could move in," Gilder said, thumbing fresh shells into his weapon.

Shawn agreed. "I expect we'll be hearing him sing out pretty quick."

"Drove them goddam buzzards off a mite, too."

His own pistol again ready, Starbuck looked skyward. The vultures had withdrawn a considerable distance. That worry should end soon now. Brandon would signal and the outlaws would either be his captives or his victims and no longer a threat. Either way they could soon remove Rome and Moody from the, plateau.

The minutes dragged on and the signal did not come. A quarter-hour passed. Starbuck and Gilder, holding their fire for fear of hitting the lawman, waited restlessly among the rocks. Once again the buzzards began to drift in. The quarter-hour became a full half.

Abruptly Shawn came to his feet. "Something's gone wrong," he said in a tight voice. "You keep watching— I'm going down there."

CHAPTER 14

WHEN HARRY BRANDON STEPPED INTO THE BRUSH fringing the rocky plateau, he paused and looked back. Starbuck and the drunk were moving up to where they could see the coulee where Ollie Kastman and Snow were waiting. They had a moment's conversation and then Starbuck fired his pistol, drawing reply from the rifles below.

Brandon grinned, bobbed his head in satisfaction. So far his plan had worked perfectly except for that one little error—his putting a bullet in Charlie Cole and killing him. That hadn't been just exactly the way he'd set it up, but he guessed it didn't matter; it all worked out to the same end.

Moving on, he began to pick his route down the steep slope. Within a dozen strides he was soaking wet from the waterlogged brush and the still dripping trees, but he gave it no thought. Soon it would all be behind him. He'd be a rich man, taking it easy, enjoying life.

Abruptly his feet went out from under him as he trod upon an unusually slippery patch of soil. He went down hard, jarring a curse from his lips, but he was unhurt, only thoroughly muddied, and he quickly resumed the descent.

He'd fooled them all—the town, the mining company, the posse, and he was about to top it off by outsmarting his own partners. No one would ever know what really had happened there in the rocks and the coulee they overlooked, and while the search party that would eventually come upon the scene was trying to puzzle it out, he'd be somewhere deep in Mexico soaking up sunshine, rolling in luxury and living the sort of life he'd often dreamed of but had entertained small hope of ever achieving.

Halting to catch his breath, he steadied himself against a juniper. Gunshots racketed again across the slope. The sound revived the smile on his lips and, pleased, he spent a few moments smoothing his heavy mustache. Starbuck and Gilder were following his orders to the letter, and Kastman and Ben Snow were shooting back just as he'd instructed them to do.

He continued on, mind turning now to the past. He'd had plans then, too, big plans to make something of his life, of stepping up from a lowly town marshal in a place such as Wolf Crossing to a position of wearing the badge in a larger settlement.

From there he would go on to take over the star in an

even larger town, become a sheriff with power reaching throughout an entire county. And then it would be a U. S. marshal's job and he'd be a federal officer.

But it hadn't worked out that way, and piece by piece, he'd lost the dream. He could never seem to rise above the little one-horse dumps like Wolf Crossing and take that first, long step up to a bigger, more important position.

Then one day he realized it was too late. He'd become too old and deep inside him was a voice saying that he wasn't good enough anymore to do the job that even a small town expected.

Harry Brandon had made up his mind at that point; he couldn't reach the goal he'd set for himself, no matter how hard he tried, by doing it one way, so he'd turn his efforts toward attaining it in another. The opportunity presented itself not too long after he had come to that decision.

Word had come to him privately from the Paradise Mine authorities of a special shipment of gold being transported secretly to Dodge City by four men who would be posing as engineers; he, as a lawman, was asked to see to any needs they might develop.

He'd seen to needs, all right—his own. He'd sent word to Dodge, where he knew Ollie Kastman was dealing faro in one of the saloons, instructed him to recruit two or three dependable partners and meet him at a deserted cabin not far out of Wolf Crossing. Ollie had been a shotgun rider for one of the stage coach lines and more or less understood the problems and drawbacks of packing a star, only he'd been smart enough to chuck it all and take up a more lucrative way of making a living.

Kastman had shown up with two friends, as directed, and he'd outlined his plan, it being that they were to ambush the four supposed engineers, relieve them of the gold and flee southward on the trail that cut through the mountains. To make it look good and to circumvent the entry of any outside law forces, he would follow with a small posse, lead them into a second ambush, after which the four of them would split the gold and go their separate ways.

They would have plenty of time to make an escape because it would likely be a week, perhaps even two, before someone finally decided to organize a search party and go looking for the posse.

Everything worked out just as he'd planned, even to the posse. The town had played right into his hands; he'd asked for help, and feeling as they did about him and the Paradise Mine people, they'd turned their backs on him and there'd been no volunteers except the black man, the greenhorn and Dave Gilder, who'd do anything for the price of a drink.

At that point he'd acted on a hunch. The three who had agreed to ride with him weren't impressive enough; he needed someone in the party with a little higher standing. Starbuck, who had the look of a gunslinger and the manner of a straight-down-the-line sort of U.S. marshal he'd once hoped to be, came drifting into town at that moment and he'd persuaded him to join up.

But now he was thinking that could be his one mistake. Starbuck was pretty much living up to the impression he gave. He was no ordinary saddlebum and he wasn't going to be fooled easily, but so far he'd posed no big problem. There'd been some opposition on his part, none of which was serious—and in a few more minutes it wouldn't make any difference. He'd be dead just like all the others.

Two down and two to go—insofar as the posse was

concerned. The nigger had been cut down by Kastman and Snow when held tried to cross the ridge—no thanks to Starbuck. And too bad it hadn't been him, but he was too smart to fall for that order. It would have been comforting to get the tall rider out of the way.

And that damned fool greenhorn, as loco as they get for some reason, had obliged by trying to reach the black and drag him off the ridge—thus there were only Gilder and Starbuck to account for. Gilder would be a cinch, but Starbuck—

Brandon halted again, once more listened to a rattling exchange of gunshots. He was fairly near the coulee now, judging from the sound of the outlaws' rifles. . . . Outlaws. . . . He sleeved away the water dashed onto his face by swinging branches and reckoned he belonged in that category. But what the hell, better to be a rich, fat outlaw than an old, worn-out lawman that nobody cared a rap about.

He pushed on, moving with greater care, endeavoring to make his approach as quiet as possible. Kastman and Snow were expecting him, after which the idea was for him to signal down whatever remained of the posse—in this case Starbuck and Gilder—with the word that he had captured the outlaws and they were his prisoners.

They would all wait quietly there in the coulee until Starbuck and Dave Gilder, coming down the slope, got in range and then he and his partners would open up on them. That would mark the end of the posse.

Days—or maybe weeks—later when the search party came upon their dead bodies, it would appear to have been a showdown fight in which the forces of the law had come out second best. The fact that Charlie Cole now would be found there also would lend credence to the affair.

As for himself, the fact that his body was missing would lead to the conclusion that he had attempted to pursue the fleeing outlaws farther and was probably killed somewhere in the vast wilderness that stretched around them. They would decide it was useless to look for his body.

That was the general plan—the one concocted by him and Kastman and the two others. But Harry Brandon had a scheme of his own.

CHAPTER 15

THE COURSE BRANDON HAD TAKEN DOWN THE treacherous slope was not hard to follow; the difficulty lay in staying upright. Shawn made his way carefully—this was no time for a broken leg or arm—bracing himself whenever possible by catching onto an extending branch or a hand on a boulder.

The route was apparently a familiar one to the lawman, for not once had he ended up in any of the numerous, small, dead-end draws or been forced to backtrack after running into a butte or similar formation. It was as if he had made the descent before but that was not likely, Starbuck was sure. The area was far removed from Wolf Crossing, and while Brandon did profess to be familiar with the country, his knowledge would be confined to the trail itself.

Brandon's tracks began to veer right, taking a circular course about midway of the slope. Shawn paused, to catch up with his labored breathing. He could not be far from the coulee and it was best he proceed henceforth with caution. He was certain now that the marshal had walked into a trap, was either in bad trouble or dead. Far too much time had elapsed since he left the crowning rocks of the slope and started down the grade for the hiding outlaws.

Breath recovered, Starbuck moved on, placing each booted foot carefully, choosing his own path now while his eyes searched the brush ahead for signs of the clearing where the outlaws were making their stand, and his ears strained for any sounds that would warn him.

He reached a roll in the land, again halted. Wet to the skin, he was cold there in the shadows of the trees where the sun could not find its way. Rubbing his hands together, he looked back up the slope. He could see the ledge-like pile of rocks where Dave Gilder waited and a section of the slope directly below it. Like the plateau where Able Rome and Walt Moody had died, it was open ground with only a few small rocks and stringy clumps of brush to break its steep surface.

He was no more than halfway to the coulee, he realized, gauging the probable location from its remembered position below the summit. At once he resumed the descent, pushed now by a strong sense of urgency to reach the clearing, convinced that something was wrong.

At quickened pace he hurried down the slope, taking longer strides, slipping, sliding, catching himself time after time. Twice he went to his knees, saved himself from falling completely by clutching at the brush.

"Starbuck—Gilder!"

The shout brought him to a quick stop. Brandon's voice came from a considerably lower level on the slope and well to his right.

"Come on down here and help me. . . . I got 'em cold!"

Shawn heaved a deep sigh. The marshal was all right.

93

Apparently he had managed to close in on the two outlaws and capture them without firing a shot. Glancing to the crest of the slope, he saw Dave Gilder silhouette briefly against the skyline and then move forward to start the descent to the coulee.

Pulling out his handkerchief, Starbuck dried his face and moved on. There was no great hurry now to reach the clearing. Brandon had everything under control.

Abruptly a half-dozen gunshots shattered the stillness of the mountainside. Starbuck wheeled, looked toward the rocks. Dave Gilder was down, rolling frantically to reach the safety of a mound of weedy earth. Bullets were digging into the soil around him, sending up small spurts of sand.

It could mean only one thing; the outlaws had somehow overcome Brandon, had opened up on Gilder with their rifles when he started toward them in obedience to the lawman's summons. They had overlooked one thing—him.

Grim, he drew his pistol and headed off along the slope at a run. The location of the coulee was established in his mind now, thanks to Brandon's yell and the gunshots, and he need waste no time searching for it; he had only to bear straight on the slanting course he was taking and be led to it.

In that next instant Shawn felt his feet shoot out from under him. For a fraction of time he seemed suspended in midair, and then he struck hard. Breath gushed from his lips as he slid into the unyielding trunk of a deep-rooted pine. Lights popped before his eyes as his head thudded into a half-buried ledge of granite. . . . And then all was in darkness.

Harry Brandon hunched low in the brush that skirted the

94

coulee. He could hear Ben Snow and Kastman talking but their voices were low, guarded, and he could not make out the words.

He drew his pistol, examined it, making sure no mud had become jammed in its muzzle during his passage down the slope. It was clean, and shoving it back into its holster, he stood upright.

"Ollie," he called softly.

"Here."

The reply came at once. Brandon stepped forward, taking no pains to conceal his approach, and entered the clearing.

"Keep your head down!" Kastman warned hastily. "Them friends of your's've done killed old Charlie. Shoot at everything that moves."

Brandon moved in behind the two men, took up a position between and slightly to the rear.

"Was wondering which one of you it was. Deputy jumped the gun on me, started shooting before I could stop him. Sure hate it."

"So does Charlie," Ben Snow said laconically. "We was expecting you sooner."

"It was that damned storm—and then one of them fool posse members fell down the side of the mountain. Had to waste time dragging him back up. . . . Everything all set?

"Just waiting on you to give the word," Kastman replied. "Horses and mules are right down the trail a piece."

"What're we doing about Charlie?" Snow, a scarred, dark-faced man with a week's growth of beard on his jaws, asked.

"Leaving him lay," Brandon said promptly. "Makes it look like there was a real, stem-winder of a hoedown between the posse and you—us. Two dead men up there on the ridge, be two more on the slope and him down here. Works out good."

"That all of the posse that's left—two?"

Brandon nodded. "Was only me and four of them to start with."

Ben Snow chuckled. "Nailing them two was like picking off them little ducks in a shooting gallery, way they was running across there."

Brandon glanced at the sun. "Reckon we'd best get things going. I'll sing out, like I told them I would, and they'll start coming down the slope. That's when you open up."

"You just get on with your signaling," Snow said. "Me'n Ollie'll do the rest."

Brandon pulled back a step to where the brush would conceal him, and drawing his pistol with his right hand, cupped the left to his mouth.

"Starbuck—Gilder! Come on down here and help me. . . . I got em cold!"

He remained motionless until he saw the first figure step into view at the edge of the rocks and start down the slope. Gilder, he thought. Starbuck would probably show up at the opposite end of the pile.

Abruptly Ben Snow began to fire. Kastman also opened up. He saw Gilder stumble and fall, then scramble on all fours to reach cover. Starbuck—where the hell was that goddam Starbuck?

There was no time to wait, to wonder where he was or curse his two partners for not holding off until both men were in view. Starbuck could have taken it upon himself to follow him down the east side of the mountain. It would be like the sonofabitch to cross him that way. Regardless—there was no time to lose.

Crouching, he brought his weapon to bear on Ollie Kastman's broad back. He pressed off a shot. The impact of the bullet at such close range drove the man forward, knocked him sprawling into the clearing beside Charlie Cole.

Snow, still levering shots at Gilder, paused, half turned. His features were blanked with surprise and fear.

"Hey—?" he said in a high pitched voice. "What the hell—"

Brandon's second bullet caught him in the right breast, slammed him into the stump next to which he was sitting.

His mouth pulled into a hard, tight line, Harry Brandon drew back farther into the brush, ears straining to pick up any noise that would tell him of Starbuck's location, if he was nearby. There was only silence.

He swore feelingly. Starbuck had screwed up his plans but good! He was supposed to be laying dead there on the slope with Gilder—dead as the two whose job it was to kill them. Why the hell hadn't he stayed put like he was told, and then come down the slope with that lousy drunk of a Gilder the way it had been planned? All that careful scheming blown to hell. . . .

Brandon shook his head. There was no use getting all spooked over it. It wasn't that serious. He'd simply wait for Starbuck to show up, then put a bullet in him same as he had Ollie and Ben Snow.

He frowned, giving that thought. Maybe that wasn't the best thing to do; maybe it would be smarter to get the horses and the pack mules and move on. That way he could settle with Starbuck, who was sure to follow, in his own time and on his terms. Waiting there at the clearing could be risky. He'd have to watch all sides, never being sure just which way Starbuck, a tricky bastard if ever he saw one, would move in from.

No, best to move out, grab whichever of the horses looked good, and with the pack animals, head south with the gold—the whole hundred thousand dollars worth. . . . My God, a man could hardly realize just how much money that really was! A hundred thousand dollars—and it was all his just like he'd planned it would be.

Stepping forward, he snatched up the rifle that had fallen from Ben Snow's hands. A long gun would be better to use on Starbuck; it would give him distance as well as greater accuracy. He wheeled, started down the trail at a run. A good headstart on Starbuck would help, too, afford him time to pick a spot where he could pull in, set up an ambush.

CHAPTER 16

STARBUCK PICKED HIMSELF UP SLOWLY. DAZED, HE looked about, shook his head in an effort to dispel the mist shrouding it. He had been unconscious for only a few minutes, he guessed, and he seemed unhurt except for a tenderness along his left temple. Lucky. . . . He could have collected a broken bone or two as reward for his haste.

He looked down at the pistol, still held tight in his hand. It was smeared with mud. Taking out his spare bandana, he wiped it clean, made sure the barrel was not clogged. He frowned, again shook his head. . . . The forty-five—why was he holding it? In that next moment it all came rushing back to him.

Mind functioning properly again, he swung his eyes to the slope below the rocks. Dave Gilder was no longer

98

in sight, had evidently made his way to the side of the grade where more brush was available for cover. Whether he was alive or not was a question.

And Brandon. . . . At once he moved off, taking slow, careful steps. The muscles of his legs were trembling but he pushed on, the feeling that he was needed in the clearing a driving force that pushed aside the uncertainty gripping his body.

He reached the point near which he thought the coulee lay, halted, listened intently. Off to the right he heard a faint rasping sound. Dropping low, he made his way forward until he gained the brush that encircled the area of open ground. There, pistol once more in hand, he stopped short. Three bodies lay in the coulee. Harry Brandon's was not one of them.

Giving that a moment's consideration, he called softly: "Marshal?"

There was no response. He repeated the summons in a louder voice.

"Starbuck—that you?"

It was Dave Gilder. Shawn wheeled to the slope. "Here," he said, and hurried through the undergrowth to the upper edge of the clearing.

Gilder, his neckerchief knotted about his left leg at a point just above the knee, struggled to an upright position as Shawn approached. His eyes were bright and there was a grimness to his mouth.

"What the hell's happened down there?"

"Three dead men,—" Starbuck replied. "Brandon's not among them. You hit bad?"

"Bullet went clean through, missed the bone," Gilder said, pulling at the makeshift bandage. "I can manage."

Shawn glanced up the slope. "You crawl all the way to here?"

Dave nodded. "Figured the marshal was in trouble and I'd best get here to help fast as I could. Just made it when I heard you calling him. Where you reckon he is?"

Starbuck shifted his gaze to the clearing. "Something I'd like to know," he said thoughtfully.

"Could be dead—laying off in the brush somewheres."

"Just what I was thinking. I'll have a look around. Wait here—best you stay off that leg."

Gilder shrugged. "No, I reckon I can get about all right."

Shawn studied the man for a moment. It came to him again that this was a different Dave Gilder from the one he'd ridden out of Wolf Crossing with.

"Suit yourself," he said. "Best we do it quiet, however. I'm beginning to wonder about something."

Gilder pulled off his hat, ran a hand through his shock of red hair. "What's that?"

"I'd as soon not say until I'm sure. I don't like having to eat my own words if I'm wrong—which I'm hoping I am."

They separated, Dave, hobbling painfully, going to the right, Starbuck to the left. They probed the coulee's brushy perimeter, turned up no sign of the lawman. Rejoining, the two men moved then into the clearing. Tight-lipped, Starbuck crossed to the side of the nearest outlaw, rolled him to his back. It wasn't Ben, but to make doubly certain, he knelt, looked close at the eyebrows. There was no scar. He glanced at the two other bodies, neither of which remotely resembled his brother, breathed a sigh of relief. Brandon had just suckered him into joining up—

"This one's still alive!"

Starbuck came about. Gilder, on his knees, was

100

supporting the outlaw's head and shoulders and reaching for a half-empty bottle of whiskey standing against a nearby stump. Shawn picked up the liquor, and dropping to a crouch, forced a drink between the man's lips. The outlaw gagged, shuddered. His eyes opened.

He stared up at Starbuck and Gilder. The slackness in his features hardened, became angry planes. "That goddam . . . Brandon. . . ."

Shawn leaned nearer to catch the faltering words. "Where is he?"

"Run . . . for it. . . . Double-crossed me . . . and Ben. . . . Took . . . the gold."

"Double-crossed?" Gilder echoed. "You telling us that Harry Brandon was in on the holdup and killings?"

The outlaw coughed. Blood dribbled from one corner of his mouth. "Was him . . . setting . . . . it up. Sent for me . . . letter . . . in my . . . pocket."

Shawn reached into the man's shirt pocket, withdrew a soiled, folded envelope. It was addressed to Ollie Kastman, Great Western Saloon, Dodge City, Kansas. Unfolding the sheet of paper that was inside, he read it quickly and passed it to Gilder.

"Can . . . use another . . . drink."

Shawn took up the bottle and helped the outlaw down a second portion of the liquor. Kastman's eyes were glazing but he managed a weak smile.

"Obliged . . . to you."

Starbuck bent over the man. "This ambush Brandon's idea, too?"

Kastman moved his head with effort. "Was . . . to wipe out . . . the posse. Wanted to make . . . it look like . . . a big shoot-out. Aimed . . . to swap duds with one of . . . you so's nobody'd know . . . he was in . . . on it."

Gilder had finished the letter, was returning it to its envelope. Starbuck shook Kastman gently.

"Where were you going then?"

"South . . . Mexico."

"You figure that's where Brandon's headed?" Dave asked, thrusting the letter into his own pocket.

"Sure. . . . No place else . . . to go."

Undoubtedly Ollie Kastman was right, Shawn thought, except for one thing; Brandon would not be lining out straight for Mexico just yet. He had rid himself of his partners and the necessity to share the gold, but not all of the posse members were dead, as he'd planned. He would have noticed that only Dave Gilder appeared on the slope to face the bullets of the outlaw rifles and that would have stirred up a strong worry within him.

Only with everyone involved dead could he feel safe, and he would set about to repair the hitch that had developed in his scheme. Somewhere close by, Harry Brandon was waiting to finish what he had started.

Starbuck turned his attention back to Kastman. The outlaw was sucking for breath, his features again slack.

"Your horses and the pack mules—where'd you leave them?"

"On the trail . . . below a ways. . . . A drink . . . like to have . . . one more."

Gilder took up the bottle quickly, held it to Kastman's mouth, watched him gulp the fiery liquid. When he had taken sufficient, he shook his head.

"Obliged again. . . . You going. . . after Harry?"

Shawn said, "No choice."

"Good. . . . The sonofabitch's got it . . . coming to him. . . . Man can't . . . play both sides . . . of the . . . table."

102

The outlaw's words faded into silence. Dave Gilder hunched low over him, drew back.

"Dead," he said. "Wonder he lived long as he did. Brandon must've been standing right behind him when he put that bullet in his back."

Starbuck drew himself upright. In the sky above the rocky plateau the buzzards were circling low, bolder now that there was no more shooting and they no longer saw movement along the slope. He faced Gilder.

"There'll be two horses around here somewhere, if Brandon didn't drive them off. I'll take one, go after him—he'll be ahead of us on the trail, I figure. You take the other, go up and get Rome and Moody, and our own animals, make camp here."

Gilder nodded, pointed at the outlaws. "What about them?"

"Wrap them in their blankets and we'll tote them back to town, same as we'll be doing Rome and Moody."

Gilder smiled grimly. "Be quite a sight, us riding down the street, packing all them bodies—"

"I'm hoping you're right—that it'll be the two of us and not just you."

"Same here," Gilder said, sobering. "How long you want me to wait?"

"If I've got Brandon figured, he'll be holed up somewhere along the trail, watching for me to show— he's looking for me because he thinks everybody else is dead. And he won't go far before he sets his ambush. With luck I ought to be back by sundown."

Gilder bobbed his head. "I'll be here," he said, throwing a glance at the buzzards. "Let's find them horses. Want to get up to the rocks before them carrion eaters take a notion to light."

CHAPTER 17

THE TRACKS LEFT BY BRANDON'S HORSE AND THE TWO pack mules carrying the gold were clear in the soft mud of the trail, and Starbuck had no difficulty in following.

But the need for caution was apparent and he held the pursuit to a slow walk. Brandon would be expecting him, thus every bend in the path, every clump of dense brush and pile of rocks along its twisting course could prove to be the point where the lawman turned outlaw could be lying in ambush for him.

Several times Shawn halted to listen, hoping to pick up the sound of the moving animals, but on each occasion there were only the usual, everyday noises of the high hills. Brandon had gotten a good start on him and it quickly became apparent that he was pushing on steadily to maintain that lead.

Late in the afternoon he drew to a halt at the foot of a long grade. The black he had appropriated was tired and he wished now he had taken the time to get the sorrel, but at that moment he had expected to overtake Harry Brandon much sooner.

Dismounting, he stepped ahead on the trail, examined it briefly, reassuring himself that he was still on the right track, and then crossed to a mound of earth and rock covering the partly exposed roots of a wind-capsized fir. Climbing to its top, he looked out over the land, now beginning to shadow as the day lengthened.

To his left the slope dropped sharply into a deep canyon; to the right it lifted up in an almost perpendicular wall thinly populated by scrubby junipers, mountain mahogany, pines and spruce.

Starbuck nodded grimly. Brandon's escape route was

also his trap; the trail he followed was like an eyebrow on the face of the massive hill, and there was no turning off; he could do nothing but continue on its narrow width and hope to reach a suitable place where a stand could be made.

That could take days, Shawn realized. He swore wearily, another sidetrack, another delay in his search for Ben. It seemed he was forever becoming involved in the problems of others while seeking only to fulfill his own obligations. . . . But this had been a little different from usual. There had been the possibility of one of the outlaws being his missing brother. He had doubted it from the beginning, but he had felt, nevertheless, that he should be certain.

He supposed he could have pulled out back at the coulee when he had seen with his own eyes that Ben Snow was not Ben Starbuck. His personal interest and reason for being a member of Brandon's posse had ended at that moment.

But the thought had not occurred to him. His mind had been crowded with the memory of Able Rome and Walt Moody lying dead on a plateau while vultures circled patiently overhead, and the knowledge that they were there because a man who wore a star had used his good offices and the prestige of the law to flaunt his trust to satisfy personal greed.

No man could turn his back on that. Others were dead, the law had been broken by one entrusted with its upholding; it was imperative, therefore, that he be caught, returned and brought to justice. Otherwise the sacred tablet of principles by which all lived would be damaged and thereby lessened.

But why was he always the one to find himself jockeyed into a position of assuming such responsibilities? Starbuck had often pondered that question when he found himself deeply involved. Why could he never find it in himself to ride on, look to his own problem?

Shawn Starbuck had never found an answer—nor did he lose any sleep over it. Perhaps it was his upbringing at the hands of iron-willed old Hiram Starbuck to whom there were only two factors deserving consideration in this life—right and wrong. A thing was either white or it was black and there were no shadings of gray; and while that somewhat uncharitable philosophy had been tempered in Shawn by circumstance from time to time, the basic honesty of it still burned within him and adherence to it was second nature.

He moved off the mound, slipping and sliding a bit on the mud, and returned to his horse. The short rest had helped the black some, but he was in poor condition at best and Starbuck knew he could expect little from the animal. There was but one consolation; the horse Brandon was riding, also one of the outlaw's string, would be in no better shape and thus, in that respect, they were on equal footing.

It ended with that, Starbuck thought as he swung back onto the saddle and continued up the trail. Harry Brandon had all the advantages. He was somewhere ahead and on a higher elevation that permitted him to look back—and down, simplifying the task of keeping an eye out for anyone following.

Thus he could exercise judgment, either finding eventually a suitable place to halt, set up an ambush or simply continue on, mile after mile, maintaining his distance, and hope to wear down anyone pursuing him and finally lose them.

It was difficult to predict which course Brandon

would choose. Probably he would elect to kill—to stop once and for all time anyone seeking to track him down and bring him to justice. Using his gun as a means for accomplishment meant nothing to him, as the murders of his partners proved, and he doubtless would feel more secure in the knowledge that no one who had witnessed his sanguinary acts still lived.

The timber was thinning. They were again moving into high country where there was less brush growth and more firs and spruces interspersed with groves of white-trunked, golden-leafed aspens.

He realized he could no longer rely on the protection of trees that before had more or less obscured the trail, and he began to ride nearer the inside edge of the rough pathway, seeking to make himself a less visible target.

The day was growing late and darkness would be of help, but there was little he could do to take advantage of it. With the sorrel under him he could have kept moving, climbing, certain that Brandon had been forced to halt for the night; the poor condition of the black ruled out the possibility of his use. Head low, laboring with each step, he would have to rest soon or cave in.

Shawn brushed his hat to the back of his head and stared up-trail. He could see short stretches of open ground now through the scattered trees, but there was no sign of Harry Brandon.

Twice Brandon had caught a glimpse of the man so relentlessly dogging his tracks. It was Starbuck, he knew. It could be no one else. Able Rome and the greenhorn, Moody, were dead. He'd seen Gilder go down when Snow and Kastman opened up on him with their rifles. He, too, was dead or badly wounded. Therefore it had to be the big drifter. He swore harshly.

107

Why the hell couldn't his luck have held and Starbuck headed down that slope with Gilder like he was told to do instead of going off on some idea of his own! Then it would have worked out just as he'd planned.

But he reckoned he should be satisfied that only one slip had developed in his carefully plotted scheme—and a minor one at that. He was still holding all the high cards despite Starbuck, and when the proper time came, that moment when he could be absolutely sure, he'd play the ace that would end the game and set him free to enjoy the new life he longed for.

He threw a glance at the pack mules. They were barely moving, making their displeasure evident, as mules would do, at being forced to continue when they were tired and believed they had done enough for one day. He'd make them keep moving until dark, then pull in. The horse he was riding was in a hell of a shape, too.

He gauged the sun. Still another hour or so until it set—and that much time, more or less, would put him pretty well up on the summit at that flat place that was a good spot for camp as well as offering a position from which a man, so desiring, could make mighty good use of a rifle.

Harry grinned, rubbed at the side of his head in a satisfied way. . . . He'd never forget the look on Ben Snow's face back there in the coulee when he turned and saw that six gun pointing at him! Surprised just wasn't a good enough word for it.

He supposed he ought to feel a little guilty about double-crossing him and Ollie and Charlie Cole. They had pitched right in with him on the scheme and not only done a good job of grabbing the gold and taking it to the agreed-upon rendezvous, but had followed out an his instructions—even to firing a bullet into the fire that

108

first night to let him know they were just ahead and on schedule—just as he had directed.

But a man couldn't afford to get soft-hearted when it came to staking his claim on a fortune. He had to think only of himself and make plans accordingly. Hell, there wasn't any big loss, anyway! All three of them were living on borrowed time. Sooner or later they were bound to get themselves killed off.

He reckoned he was entitled to a pat on the back; everything had worked out fine when you considered it, except for Starbuck. If he was to fault himself on any one thing, he guessed it was for misjudging him and talking him into riding with the posse. But he did need one man a cut better than the three who'd volunteered, and he was the only available prospect. How was he to know Starbuck wasn't just another saddle-tramp, anyway?

Harry Brandon shrugged, spat. The hell with hashing over Starbuck. He'd take care of him, come dark, and that would be the end of it. What if he had made a little mistake and was being pushed a bit when he'd planned on being able to take his time, just fade out, vanish? It would all work out to the same end in the long run.

There was one thing that would pose a bit of a problem, once Starbuck was taken care of; he had no grub. Moving out in a hurry the way he'd been forced to do in the coulee, he'd had no time to grab the supplies Kastman and the others had been carrying. He didn't know whose horse he'd taken, but it wasn't the one packing the grub. He'd get by, however. He'd kill himself a rabbit or one of the numerous tassle-eared squirrels he'd noticed running around under the trees. That would keep him going until he reached one of the Mexican settlements he knew he'd find once the ridge was topped out and he dropped into the valley country on the other side. What the hell—for a hundred thousand dollars in gold a man could afford to go hungry for a couple of days!

The mules began to hold back. He halted, again looked to the sun. He could stop anytime now, he decided, swinging his gaze about. A hundred yards farther, a small flat, covered with thin grass and bordered on two sides with boulders, caught his attention. It was exactly what he had been looking for.

Goading the horses and yanking impatiently on the mules' lead rope, he moved into the clearing and stopped. Immediately the smaller mule lay down, ears slung forward, eyes half shut in a stubborn declaration of no further work.

Brandon, ignoring the brute, led the horse to a nearby stump, picketed him and the two pack animals. Wheeling, he jerked Ben Snow's rifle from the saddle boot and doubled back across the small flat to the ledge of rocks at its lower end. Pulling himself up onto the highest point, he looked down onto the trail.

For a time he saw nothing and the thought came to him that Starbuck had given up after all and was returning to Wolf Crossing. That set up a disturbance within him at once; he didn't want it that way; the final success of his plan depended on there being no survivors of the ambush. That damned Starbuck—a man couldn't figure—

A grunt of satisfaction slipped through his lips. A solitary rider had come into view, rounding a bulge of rock on the trail far below. It took only a few moments' steady observation to verify the identity; it was Starbuck, as he had been sure it would be.

Flattening himself, he rested the rifle on a slight

hump in the storm-scoured surface of the ledge and sighted in on the next open area in the trail that Starbuck would shortly be entering. . . . A long shot but an easy one.

Settled and waiting, Brandon glanced back to the clearing. The smaller mule, apparently concluding that his day's labor was finally over, had gotten to his feet and was now grazing contentedly alongside his associate. It would be a good idea to pull off the pack saddles for the night, give the contrary bastards a good night's rest, Harry Brandon thought. Like as not their loads hadn't been off their backs since they left the Paradise Mine. . . . Besides, he wanted a look at that gold and run his fingers over its smooth softness—and, by God, he just might eat a little of it! Yes sir, he'd shave a bit off one of the bars and swallow it so's he could tell around that he'd eaten gold. . . . That would open some eyes.

He shifted his attention back to the trail. Starbuck was still hidden from view by an outward swing of the slope. . . . That was something else he would do, actually must do—go down to where Starbuck would be lying and get rid of the body. It wouldn't do to have him found by a search party, so it would be into the canyon for him, where the buzzards and the coyotes could take care of the remains. The horse he'd keep. Between it and the jughead he was riding he might have the makings of one good animal.

There he was—Starbuck. Brandon levered the rifle, checked to be certain a live cartridge was in the chamber. He wished he'd brought his own weapon. This one of Snow's was an old Henry whereas the one he packed and was accustomed to was a later model Winchester. But it didn't matter; a rifle was a rifle and

111

one make would kill a man as dead as another. Drawing a bead on the approaching rider, he caught his breath and squeezed off a shot.

CHAPTER 18

STARBUCK, HUNCHED FORWARD ON THE PLODDING black, stared moodily at the steep rise in the trail ahead. He had expected Brandon to make his stand before this; could he be wrong about what the man had in mind? Was he going to just keep running, hope to wear out any pursuit?

It didn't seem logical. For him to believe he could push on without a break made little sense. Slowed by the two pack mules, he would know that he could not outdistance another rider not so encumbered.

A puff of smoke blossomed from the rim of a rock ledge near what appeared to be a crest. In that same particle of time the black faltered. Realization hit Shawn as the animal started to fall. Brandon! Ambush! He reacted instinctively. Kicking his feet free of the stirrups, he threw himself from the saddle as the flat, cracking sound of the rifle floated hollowly through the canyon.

Dirt spurted from the wall of the low embankment beside him as a second bullet dug into it. But Starbuck was already plunging into the thin brush and racing for the protection of a pine a dozen strides up the slope. He gained the thick-trunked tree, and gasping for wind, hunched behind it.

Jerking off his hat, he looked to the top of the trail. He could see Brandon, a vague shape in the darkening day, barely visible on a ledge of rocks that overlooked the land below. Evidently he was uncertain whether he had scored with his two bullets or not, since there had been no third. The long shadows undoubtedly were hindering his vision.

Starbuck swore harshly. That first bullet had been close. Only the fact that Brandon had slightly miscalculated in his aiming, and the black's bobbing head coming up at the exact moment it did, had saved his life.

But it was over now—all the tense watching and waiting for him to stop and make a fight of it. He was there, sprawled high in the rocks. The chase was finished.

Shawn's left hand dropped to the pistol on his hip. Drawing it, he checked its loads, found the cylinder ready except for the one chamber reserved for the hammer. Thumbing a cartridge from his belt, he filled it. It could come down to the point where his life depended on that one extra bullet.

Again he looked to the ledge. Brandon had not stirred, was still watching the trail. He held the upper hand and knew it. Up higher where he could see well, and with a far-ranging rifle, he was in control.

Starbuck sank to a crouch, made a studied survey of the hillside beyond the pine, the trail and the slope falling away from it. Trying to approach Brandon by the narrow path was out of the question; to attempt to reach him by working his way up through the scanty growth of the lower slope might be possible, but the odds were against it.

He shifted his attention back to the lifting hillside where the pine had given him safety. Its rise was steep and here cover was also scarce—but it was possible to climb. By holding to an almost direct, straight-up course

113

he could gain a rocky outcrop that paralleled the trail. He looked close, traced the ragged line of granite with his eyes. It curved away from the crest where Harry Brandon had forted himself, but it would be possible to drop from it when he drew more or less abreast that point, cross a narrow saddle and come in behind the man.

The problem would be getting up to the ledge. There was much open ground lying between his position behind the pine and the rocks. Chances that Brandon would spot him while making the climb were better than good, but once he reached the higher level it would be easy to keep out of sight. . . . And he just couldn't stay there behind the pine.

There wasn't much daylight left. What he would do must be done soon, for once night closed in, Brandon's advantage would increase. He could be sure the man would find a safe hiding place from which to protect himself on all sides—or he could even change his location completely, move on for a distance. Then it would all have to be done over again—the search, the pursuit during which he would never know when Brandon would halt, turn his rifle upon him and perhaps, this time, not miss.

Jaw set, Starbuck came to decision. He glanced once more to the summit of the trail. Brandon had pulled himself to hands and knees striving for a better view. Shawn wished briefly for a rifle of his own and then, dismissing that obviously impossible hope, bent low and pulled away from the protection of the pine. If Brandon would only keep his eyes on the trail, not permit them to stray to probe the adjacent land, all would go well. . . .

He came to a stop behind a clump of scrub oak as a thought came to him. Keeping the man's attention

114

elsewhere was the answer. Glancing about, he located a cup-sized rock. Picking it up, he moved a few steps farther until the pine no longer blocked his way to the trail. Then, putting all his strength into it, he threw the stone as hard as he could.

It fell on the slope on the far side of the trail, set up a hollow clatter. Harry Brandon pivoted on his heels. Rifle poised, he stared down into the canyon, certain now that his second bullet had not scored and that his pursuer was working his way up the steep grade below him.

Shawn waited no longer. Brandon was quartered away from him and would not shift his attention for several minutes, at least, and so the time to make the climb to the ledge with all possible speed was at hand. There was that possibility that Brandon would turn back for some reason, spot him and open up with his rifle— but it was a risk he had to take.

Bent forward, he started up the grade, keeping as low as movement permitted, assisting himself whenever opportunity presented itself by grabbing onto a bush, a rock jutting out of the dark soil, or one of the few trees that were present.

Within only a short distance he began to labor for breath as the near vertical climb took its toll of him. Once he fell, the still slippery soil giving way under him and sending him sprawling full length while a trickle of small stones rattled down the slope.

He lay motionless, certain that the racket would be heard by Brandon, but when no rifle shots came, he twisted his head, and without rising, looked to the crest of the trail. A sigh escaped him. Harry Brandon still hunched at the far end of the ledge. The falling pebbles had gone unnoticed.

Resuming his partly upright stance, Starbuck continued. The grade immediately below the rocks had become steeper and now, at closer range, he saw that what he hoped to gain was the top of a butte formation that extended shelf-like from the breast of the mountain.

The face of the escarpment was much higher than it had appeared from below and he again halted, this time from choice as he scanned the frowning, ragged wall for a break that would permit him to climb to its top.

A darkness-filled wedge lay a hundred paces to his right. It would be a wash, a spillway through which storm waters draining from upper levels poured off the shelf in their rage to reach lower ground. . . . It meant doubling back, losing precious minutes of daylight, but there was nothing else he could do.

He flung another glance at Brandon, now barely visible, and hurried on toward the gash. Cutting across the slope on a fairly level course enabled him to regain his robbed breath to some extent, and when he finally reached the break in the bluff, he was not heaving so hard and the paining of his leg muscles had lessened considerably.

The opening in the rocky wall was only a little less steep than the slope itself, but by wedging his feet against the water-smoothed rocks protruding from either side and clinging to others, he was able to draw himself, panting, sweating and aching from the strain, to the flat surface of the shelf.

Starbuck lay there for a full minute, recovering his wind, allowing the trembling to fade from his body. Then, rolling over, he got to hands and knees and once again looked to the rocks at the top of the trail. He swore exhaustedly. Brandon was no longer there.

CHAPTER 19

STARBUCK CRAWLED TO A HIGHER POINT ON THE LEDGE and, flat on his belly, scoured the darkening rocks for a sign of Brandon. He was not to be seen and the possibility that he had moved on again came to mind.

It seemed unlikely. That he had started down the trail with the thought of getting a shot at the man he believed was climbing the slope, or had simply pulled back from the shelf to a more advantageous position, made better sense.

Regardless, Shawn knew he must continue although he would again be going up against the man and his rifle blindly, not knowing where or when to expect him—and this time with the further handicap of darkness. He shrugged, swore quietly; nothing was ever easy, it seemed—and the job had to be done. Glancing again to the rocks, now almost wholly dark, he got to his feet, and remembering to keep well back from the edge of the ledge along which he moved, hurried on.

He came to the swale that separated the butte from the summit of the trail. There was no break in the wall, and reluctant to spend any time searching for one, he crossed to the edge, chose what appeared to be a fairly level section on the ground below, one devoid of rocks, and jumped.

It was a good fifteen-foot drop. He struck on the balls of his feet and, off balance because of the slanting grade, plunged forward and went to his knees. But he was up instantly, unhurt, and hurried on.

He went down the near side of the saddle, taking pains only to be as quiet as possible, and started up the opposite slope. Shortly the rocks crowning the crest

117

became more distinct and he slowed his pace. Harry Brandon could have returned; it would be wise to approach with care until he was sure of just where the man might be.

He paused, gave that consideration. It would also be smart to come in from the back side of the plateau. At once he cut to the right, made a circle of the crest, halting when he reached a patch of junipers and oak brush at its lower end. Gauging the distance to the rocks, he dropped low and worked toward the opposite edge of the springy growth, listening intently as he slowly progressed.

A horse stamped wearily, blew. Starbuck halted instantly. Brandon had not moved camp, had only changed his position on the rocks. He was somewhere nearby. Pistol in hand, Shawn resumed the tedious approach. The horse was off to his right, probably picketed in a clearing where there was grass to be had. On beyond that would be the slope; therefore it was reasonable to assume Brandon was to his left.

Scarcely breathing and taking each step with utmost care, Starbuck pushed on until he reached the end of the brush. Low to the ground, he peered through the filagree screen of leaves and branches. A small flat, beginning to brighten with the night's first stars, lay before him. The two mules and the horse Brandon was riding were in a small pocket of rocks and undergrowth to one side. Elsewhere there was no sign of life.

Shawn settled back on his haunches, easing the strain on his leg muscles. He could cut back, circle to where the animals were grazing, but his appearance could frighten them and cause a racket. Brandon, he thought, would be on the other side of the rocky formation that capped the forward edge of the plateau like a dull, gray tiara, still keeping watch on the trail and the slope. But there was no real assurance of that; the man could be hiding nearby, actually aware of his presence, Shawn realized, and waiting to open fire when he appeared.

Two could play the game. . . . Starbuck shifted to a more comfortable position and, weapon ready, stared out over the flat. Coyotes barked into the brightening night from somewhere high in the ridges. A pumpkin-yellow edge of the moon appeared on the eastern horizon, began to grow, and the sudden, quiet swish of wings overhead marked the swift passage of an owl. A chill, born of sunset, was moving in, settling over the land and Shawn pulled at the edges of his jacket, drew it tighter around his body.

Dave Gilder would be wondering about the delay. He had expected him to return by the end of the day, would now have assumed that something had gone wrong and could even be contemplating taking the trail himself. It would be a mistake; with Harry Brandon lying in wait with his rifle, Dave would ride straight into a bullet.

Starbuck drew himself up sharply. A dark figure separated itself from the end of the rocks, coming from a shadow-filled hollow along the fringe. Shawn understood then; Brandon had simply exchanged his position on the top of the formation to a more convenient one where he figured he'd be less likely seen but could still cover the slope and the trail.

Tense, Starbuck held himself motionless, watched the man walk slowly into the open. Apparently he had decided there was no point in further surveillance and was likely considering the wisdom of moving his camp. Muscles taut, Shawn waited, allowed the man to reach the center of the plateau where he was in full starlight.

"Brandon—"

At the sound of Starbuck's voice, Harry Brandon lurched to one side instinctively. His rifle rapped through the stillness as he fired fast from the hip. Shawn triggered a shot at the man as a bullet clipped through the oak leaves crowding about him. He saw that he had missed, and pressed off a second shot at Brandon throwing himself into the brush at the end of the rocks.

Starbuck, not about to let himself be trapped, leaped to his feet, and snapping another at the point where Harry Brandon had disappeared, raced for the massive pile of boulders. The mules and the horse were milling around anxiously, frightened by the gunshots, but they were making no effort to break loose. They were either picketed securely or hobbled.

Shawn reached the rocks, reloaded his weapon as he began to circle the formation. Brandon could only be at the opposite end or else retreating down the trail, which was not likely. He halted suddenly, ears picking up the faint scrape of boot leather against stone.

Pulling in tight against the cool granite, he hunched in the shadows, listened, striving to pin down the location of the sound. It came again—from somewhere above. Brandon was climbing to the top of the pile, hoping to catch him below.

Shawn rode out the breathless moments. There was silence again, and then once more that scraping noise. It was closer. A change came into the starlight—as if something had moved through it. He pulled back from the boulders, eyes sweeping the arcing level of the pile.

Harry Brandon, crouched, was silhouetted against the night ten paces away. Head cocked, he held his pistol ready, having given up the rifle for a more quickly managed six gun.

"Last chance, Brandon," Starbuck murmured.

"Don't—"

Brandon spun, went to one knee. The weapon in his hand burnt a small orange hole in the night in the same instant that Shawn fired. Starbuck felt a bullet whip past his arm, and fired again.

Brandon slumped forward. His gun slipped from his fingers, clattered noisily upon the rocks. He twisted half about, fought to regain his feet, fell heavily instead and rolled limply back into the clearing.

Starbuck, motionless in the pale glow, sucked in a deep breath. He had hoped to take the man to Wolf Crossing alive, but Brandon had not seen it that way. Holding his pistol in his right hand, Shawn rodded out the spent cartridges, and while tension ebbed slowly from his tall frame, reloaded.

Afterwards he circled the rocks to where Brandon lay. For a time he stared at the slack face and then, bending down, unpinned the star from the man's pocket. Dropping it into a pocket, he turned away.

The night had been long and cold and a deep thoughtfulness had weighed heavily on Shawn Starbuck. He had tried to avoid a shoot-out—twice—but Harry Brandon, aware no doubt that he had closed all gates behind him, had made his own desperate choice.

At sunup, Shawn roused from his place beside the fire he had built, and crossing to the horse Brandon had been riding, dug around in the saddlebags for food. He found none. A search of the packs the mules carried also failed to turn up anything. Brandon had departed the coulee in such haste he had neglected to take any grub—only gold.

Low in spirit and hungry, Shawn returned to the fire. He could, he supposed, take Brandon's rifle and do a bit of hunting in the grassy saddle beyond the plateau. He'd find rabbits there, he was sure, and one broiled over flames would take the edge off his need and keep him going until he could get back to camp where Dave Gilder waited.

But the idea didn't appeal to him for some reason obscure even to himself, and after a bit, he kicked out the fire, and leading the horse to where Brandon lay, he loaded the body on behind the saddle and secured it.

He turned then to the mules, made certain their loads were tiding properly, and linking the string ropes, brought them into the center of the clearing. There he mounted to the saddle. The horse grunted a little under the additional weight and Starbuck knew he was in for some walking before the return trip was over, but it didn't matter. All he wanted now was to get back to Wolf Crossing, rid himself of the unwanted responsibility that had fallen on him, and be on his way.

Moving off the flat, he swung onto the trail and started down the steep grade. A short time later he passed the horse he had been riding when Brandon's bullet had come reaching for him and found, instead, a different target, and then around noon he came into sight of the high, rock ridge where Able, Rome and Walt Moody had died.

A thin curl of smoke twisting up from the base of the slope below it told him that Gilder was still there, likely had coffee and a meal on the fire. The thought induced him to put spurs to the lagging horse and jerk impatiently at the rope leading the stolid mules.

Dave was standing at the back edge of the clearing when he rode in. Face expressionless, he made brief acknowledgment of Starbuck's greeting, touched the lifeless shape of Harry Brandon with a glance, and

122

brought his attention again to bear upon Shawn, now swinging off the saddle.

"I'm hating to do this," he said in a tight voice.

Starbuck pivoted slowly. "What's that?"

"You heard," Dave Gilder replied coolly. "I'm taking that gold."

CHAPTER 20

STARBUCK SETTLED GENTLY ON HIS HEELS, EYES ON the pistol in Gilder's white knuckled hand. The hard, crushing pressure of what he was undertaking had caused him to neglect cocking the weapon. Shawn knew the odds for him to draw his own gun and fire before Dave could correct the error were better than good. There had been enough killing—far too much, in fact.

"What the hell's this all about?"

Sweat covered Gilder's face with a wet shine. "Told you. Gold's mine. I'm taking it—clearing out."

Starbuck shook his head slowly. "Forget it. Be the biggest mistake you ever made."

"No—I made that one a long time ago—when I took my first drink. That gold's the only way I can make up for all I've done. I can square myself, get a new start."

"It's not that easy. You think it'll end here? That mining company won't ever stop hunting you."

"Won't know who to hunt for. Brandon, the posse, and them outlaws—all dead."

"I'm not."

"That there parts up to you. Drop your gun, kick it over to me."

Shawn did not move, continued to study the man. There was a sullen determination in his eyes but beneath

123

it all he detected a current of uncertainty. Dave Gilder was walking a path he never before had trod, and the tenseness of the experience was getting to him. Shrugging, Starbuck lifted his forty-five from its holster, let it fall to the ground. Gilder was still worth gambling on.

"Kick it over here."

Shawn complied, folded his arms across his chest. "What's next?"

Dave, squatting slowly, never removing his gaze from Starbuck, recovered the pistol. Straightening, he thrust it under the waistband of his faded denims.

"Up to you—I don't want to leave you laying here dead like all them others," he said, jerking a thumb at the blanket-wrapped bodies of Rome, Moody and the three outlaws lined up on the grass at the edge of the coulee. "Expect it's what I'll have to do if you ain't agreeable."

"To what?"

"Giving me your word."

The strain that gripped Gilder appeared to be tapering off as he talked. Shawn breathed a little easier.

"What's that got to do with it?"

"Everything. I want you to say you'll keep riding, not head back to Wolf Crossing and tell what happened here—and about me taking the gold."

Starbuck said, "No deal, Dave."

Gilder frowned, swallowed nervously. "Not even if I was to give you a part of the gold?"

"It'd make no difference."

Gilder forced a short laugh. "You meaning you ain't got no use for gold?"

"Sure I have—but not that kind. The blood of ten men has been spilled all over it, and that's something I'd not

124

be able to forget. Be the same for you, too, if you go through with this."

"I've got to do it!" Gilder said in a high, desperate tone. "Only way I can fix up what I've done and make it right with my wife and boys!"

"You think that going to them with your pockets full of money's going to wipe out the past? Gold's not what they want from you—it's something else and you damn well know it!"

"But with the gold I can—"

"You can't do anything with it but buy more trouble, make things worse."

Dave Gilder mulled over Shawn's words in a morose silence. One of the mules stirred restlessly, began to crop at the grass in the coulee.

"No!" Gilder said abruptly. "You ain't changing my mind. I done thought it all out. Got it figured the same as Brandon—and it'll work for me same as it would for him."

Starbuck lifted his hands, allowed them to fall in a gesture of resignation. "It means you'll have to kill me, too."

"I don't want to. You're the only man I've run up against that treated me decent. I owe you for that, but I can't let nothing stand in the way of my wife and boys. They're going to have all the things they've always wanted for and couldn't have."

"You think they'd take any of it knowing what you did to get it?"

"Won't know—"

"They will, Dave, don't fool yourself. You'll show it. You'll keep remembering those dead men laying there and you'll always be wondering if somebody's about to catch up with you and claim the gold—even kill you to

125

get it back."

"It's my only chance—hope," Gilder said doggedly.

"Wrong. You've got a different kind of a chance facing you, one that'll make your family proud of you and let you live the right kind of a life."

Gilder brushed at the sweat on his face with his free hand. "What's that mean?"

"Just this—we're the last of Brandon's posse, the only ones left. We've done what we set out to do, get back the gold that was stolen—and we've got the outlaws who did it. Going to be a big feather in your cap."

Dave laughed scornfully. "Yours—won't be in mine."

"I'm only a part of it, and a stranger to boot. You're the man they know and folks in Wolf Crossing will be looking at you different from now on."

"With all that gold I can—"

"You don't need it. You're licking your whiskey problem and won't need it for a crutch anymore, and you've proved you're as good as any man and due the respect you're bound to get now—"

"Sure'n hell can't raise a family on respect!"

"No, but you can make that respect work for you, provide you with a job that will."

Gilder wagged his head hopelessly. "Job! What kind of a job could I get—a swamper in Ed Christian's saloon?"

"That's the kind the old Dave Gilder could get but not the new one. I'm talking about the man you can be now—not the one you were."

"Still don't mean nothing to me."

"It can. Wolf Crossing needs a marshal now. You can ask to fill in till election time, then run for the job."

126

Gilder's jaw sagged. "Me? Get elected marshal? Hell, folks'd laugh themselves sick."

"Maybe a little—at first. You've got to expect that. They only remember what you were and it's up to you to prove that things have changed—that you're different now."

"You're talking loco. They'd never let me pin on that star—even if it was just till election."

"I figure they will after I tell them how you dragged yourself down that slope, shot in the leg, to help Brandon when you thought he was in trouble and needed you. That kind of proof they'll understand."

Dave Gilder's expression slowly changed. The strain faded from his features and a flicker of hope touched his eyes. "You really meaning that? You ain't just talking, saying it because I'm holding a gun on you?"

Starbuck smiled. "One that's not even cocked? Not much. I'm only saying what's the truth." He raised his hand, pointed to the blackened pot balanced over the low fire. "It's been a long night. All right if I help myself to some coffee?"

Gilder was staring at the pistol he was holding. He nodded woodenly, a strange look on his face.

Shawn stepped to the circle of stones, picked up a cup. Dumping its cold dregs, he filled it with simmering black liquid. Taking a long drink, he sighed gratefully.

"Needed that. Brandon forgot to take grub with him." Reaching into the spider sitting nearby he helped himself to several strips of fried meat and began to eat.

"It just wouldn't work out—not for me," Gilder said finally, his tone forlorn. "I know how it'd be. Nothing'll ever change."

"Nobody's saying it'll be easy. You've got a long hill to climb, but you can do it if you set your mind to it."

"And if folks let me—"

"They'll throw in with you, work with you."

"I ain't sure," Dave Gilder murmured. "And about this here marshal's job—I can see you getting elected, but me—"

"I'm out of it. I'll be gone, which leaves you the only member of the posse still in Wolf Crossing—the one man left there that got the job done. That's a big recommendation—and people won't be overlooking it."

"Seems kind of funny—me—talking about being the marshal."

"It's the chance you've been waiting for but couldn't find because you were looking for it through the bottom of a bottle. You've got rid of that bottle now, so there's nothing standing in your way."

"I ain't so sure I have—"

"You have, if you keep on believing it."

Hunkered on his heels, Starbuck stole a glance at Gilder. Dave had lowered the pistol, was staring at the ground.

"What's it to be?" he asked quietly. "Put a bullet in me, run with the gold—and spend the rest of your life waiting for a lawman or a Pinkerton detective to step out of the dark with a gun in his hand? Or do we go back to Wolf Crossing and start building a new life for you and your family?"

Gilder stirred helplessly. "I don't know. . . . I just ain't for sure about anything."

"No problem deciding which is right and which is wrong."

"No, it ain't that. It's not for sure I can do all the things you figure I can. I tried before and couldn't make it."

"That's not hard to understand. You hadn't convinced

yourself that you could—didn't believe in yourself. And a bottle was the wrong kind of courage. It's not that way now. You've already proved yourself and you've got yourself the chance to grab onto something good—a lawman's star."

Dave Gilder slid his weapon back into the holster. Taking Shawn's pistol from his waistband, he stepped up to the fire, passed it over, butt first. His eyes were solemn and there was a resoluteness to his features.

"I'll sure as hell try—"

Shawn came to his feet. "That's all any man can do," he said, and reached into his shirt pocket. Taking the star he had removed from Harry Brandon's body, he pinned it on Gilder's shirt. "You might as well get used to wearing this. I expect it's going to be yours for a long time."

Dave Gilder looked down at the emblem. His hand rose slowly. His fingers touched the cool metal, traced the lettering hesitantly. He swallowed hard.

"I—I don't know—" he mumbled. "Maybe I ought to wait—see—"

"No need. We're the only ones left of Brandon's posse, and I'm just riding through. Only right that you take charge."

Gilder gave that consideration. After a moment he nodded, smiling faintly. And then once again his features clouded.

"Only thing—what about me throwing down on you, planning to take the gold—"

Starbuck shrugged. "It's between you and me, and best forgot. Let's get these bodies loaded up and head out. . . . It's a long way back to Wolf Crossing, Marshal."

CHAPTER 21

THEY RODE INTO THE SETTLEMENT AROUND NOON, AND by the time they had led their pack train of yellow gold and lifeless bodies to a halt at the livery stable's rack, most of the town was gathered about them, peeking at the shrouded shapes in quiet awe and voicing questions in subdued voices.

Starbuck and Dave Gilder, trail-worn and stiff, dismounted and faced the stunned crowd. A man in the front, his ruddy features reflecting shock and disbelief, stared at them.

"You two the only ones left alive?"

Shawn nodded, started a reply, withheld his words as Ed Christian and four other men shouldered their way briskly through the gathering. The one to Christian's left, small, sharp-faced, with snapping dark eyes, swept the pack train with his glance, whipped it back to Starbuck and Gilder.

"I hear right—there only two of you left?"

"That's it, Mr. Stratton," Dave replied. "Just us."

"My God," Stratton breathed. "Even Brandon—"

"Even him," Gilder said, "only wasn't the way you maybe are thinking. He tried to take the gold himself. He was hooked up with them outlaws—had it all framed up. I got a letter of his proving that. He would've got away with it, too, if it hadn't been for Starbuck. He went after him, brought him and the gold both back."

A mutter of surprise ran through the crowd. Dave waited for it to die, then, looking about apprehensively, said: "I'll make a report on what happened."

Stratton bobbed his head. "Good. We'll be needing it for the town records." He broke off, eyes fixed on the

130

badge pinned to Gilder's shirt pocket. "That Brandon's star you're wearing?"

"Yes, sir. I figured the town'd need a lawman, leastwise until election. Seeing as how I've already been deputized, I'm volunteering to hold down the job—it's all right with you and the rest of the town council."

Someone in the crowd laughed. Several others took it up. Shawn threw a hasty look at Gilder, saw the lines of his face tighten, his skin grow a shade lighter. It was a critical moment, he realized.

"I'm recommending it, if what I say's worth anything to you," Starbuck said, speaking in a loud and clear voice. "If it wasn't for Dave this could've all turned out different."

Stratton shifted his attention to Ed Christian and the three men flanking him closely; evidently they were the council. All nodded.

"All right," Stratton said, coming back to Gilder. "You're the acting marshal, temporary until election time. You sure you can handle it?"

"Yes, sir, I know I can—and I'll prove it to you, to the whole town."

"You're getting your chance," Stratton said. "Now if—"

"Something else," Gilder cut in. "I'd like to say now I'll be running for the job, permanent, when it comes up for voting."

Starbuck smiled. Dave Gilder had gotten the worst part of it over—the declaring of himself—and had discovered he was still alive and breathing and none the worse for it. It would be easier for him now.

Ed Christian pushed forward, extended his hand to Gilder. "I'll tell you this, Dave, I'm for you. Call on me if you need any help."

Gilder grinned broadly. "Obliged. I expect I'll be needing a lot of it—all I can get." He lifted his gaze to cover the crowd. "I hope I can figure on you all voting for me—"

"They get the gold?"

Shawn turned to face two men moving in from the side. Both were dressed in the customary corduroy suits, lace boots and narrow-brimmed hats associated with the mining companies.

"They did," Stratton said coldly, motioning toward the pack train. As the pair hurried to reach the mules, he nodded to Shawn and Gilder. "They're from the Paradise. Been hanging around here since the day after you left. Tall one's named Blaylock—he's the superintendent. The other's Otto Bond, office manager or something like that."

He turned away then, faced the crowd. "Some of you men unload those bodies, get them over to the undertaker's. Being there in the sun ain't helping them any. Tell Amos that Doc Marberry'll be along presently and do his coroner duties. Can bury them later."

"Mr. Mayor—" Blaylock said, moving back into the center of the gathering with his partner. "I want to thank you. The gold's all there. Putting your lawmen on it quick like you did and making the recovery won't be forgotten by the Paradise Mining Company."

"There are the men to thank," Stratton replied, jerking his thumb at Starbuck and Gilder, "them and the ones that died doing it."

"Sorry about them, and like I said, we won't forget it. We aim to transfer a part of our business here as a show of appreciation—"

A cheer went up from the crowd. Blaylock raised his arms for silence.

"That's not all. There'll be a generous reward for these two men—a generous one."

Dave Gilder smiled, evidently seeing the possibilities of sending for his family growing brighter. Shawn caught at Blaylock's arm.

"I'd appreciate it if you'll just turn my part over to the marshal."

The mine superintendent frowned, puzzled. "Sure, Mr.—"

"Starbuck."

"Mr. Starbuck. Whatever you say."

Dave Gilder frowned. "No, it ain't right. I won't let—"

"It's what I want. Sooner you get your wife and boys here, the better it'll be."

Gilder looked down, murmured: "Hell, Starbuck, I don't know how to thank you."

"You know all right. We talked it all out back there in the coulee."

"I guess we did," Dave said slowly. He raised his head, nodded. "And don't worry none. I'll make it."

"I know you will," Shawn answered, and taking the sorrel's reins, started for the stable.

"Now wait, seems we ought to owe you something," Ed Christian said, halting him with an outstretched hand.

Starbuck turned to him. "Just one thing—a favor. Get folks behind Dave Gilder and elect him marshal. He'll make you a damned good one."

"We'll do it," Christian said promptly. "But what about yourself?"

Shawn brushed at the stubble on his chin. "All I want is to get cleaned up, do a bit of eating and sleeping and then I'm riding on. I got a brother somewhere. I figure

133

he could be in Santa Fe so I'm going to have a look."

Otto Bond, standing on the porch of the Grand Central that next morning with mine superintendent Joe Blaylock, watched Starbuck ride slowly down the street and disappear around the corner of the last building.

"Sure cool customer," he said. "I wish't we could get somebody like him to take over the bullion wagons."

Blaylock hawked, spat into the already dry dust. "The right kind, all right, only they never stick. Always move on—like that one we had working for a spell. Damon his name was."

"Damon," Bond repeated, frowning. "Oh, sure, I remember him now. Come to think of it, they even look something alike. You reckon they're related?"

"Names ain't the same. Don't seem likely."

"Still, he could be a relative—cousin or something."

"Yeh, suppose so. We could've asked if we'd thought."

"Just never come to me. Maybe it won't make any difference."

"Why's that?"

"I recollect Damon saying he was going on to Santa Fe when he quit. They'll probably be bumping into each other if he's still there. Santa Fe's no big town."

"No, it sure ain't. . . What do you say we eat?"

"I'm ready," Otto Bond said, and stepped down into the street.

We hope that you enjoyed reading this
Sagebrush Large Print Western.
If you would like to read more Sagebrush titles,
ask your librarian or contact the Publishers:

United States and Canada

Thomas T. Beeler, *Publisher*
Post Office Box 659
Hampton Falls, New Hampshire 03844-0659
(800) 251-8726

United Kingdom, Eire, and
the Republic of South Africa

Isis Publishing Ltd
7 Centremead
Osney Mead
Oxford OX2 0ES England
(01865) 250333

Australia and New Zealand

Australian Large Print Audio & Video P/L
17 Mohr Street
Tullamarine, Victoria, 3043, Australia
1 800 335 364